P

Carltou 111

Also by Carlton Mellick III

Satan Burger
Electric Jesus Corpse
Sunset With a Beard (stories)
Razor Wire Pubic Hair
Teeth and Tongue Landscape
The Steel Breakfast Era
The Baby Jesus Butt Plug
Fishy-fleshed
The Menstruating Mall
Ocean of Lard (with Kevin L. Donihe)
Punk Land
Sex and Death in Television Town
Sea of the Patchwork Cats
The Haunted Vagina
Cancer-cute (Avant Punk Army Exclusive)
War Slut
Sausagey Santa
Ugly Heaven, Beautiful Hell (with Jeffrey Thomas)
Adolf in Wonderland
Ultra Fuckers
Cybernetrix
The Egg Man
Apeshit
The Faggiest Vampire
The Cannibals of Candyland
Warrior Wolf Women of the Wasteland
The Kobold Wizard's Dildo of Enlightenment +2
Zombies and Shit
Crab Town
The Morbidly Obese Ninja

THE
HAUNTED
VAGINA

CARLTON MELLICK III

ERASERHEAD PRESS
PORTLAND, OREGON

ERASERHEAD PRESS
205 NE BRYANT
PORTLAND, OR 97211

WWW.ERASERHEADPRESS.COM

ISBN: 0-9762498-8-X

AUTHOR'S NOTE

I miss Andre the Giant.

- Carlton Mellick III   4/14/2011 8:48 am

CHAPTER ONE

I've been scared to have sex with Stacy ever since I discovered her vagina was haunted.

When we first met, I didn't notice her vagina was haunted at all. It seemed perfectly fine. *Better* than fine. It was great! At least, for the first year. But after we got engaged, and she moved in with me, I noticed odd sounds coming from her while she slept.

At first, I just thought it was her snoring. Then I thought there was a television left on somewhere in the house. I heard voices in the dark—whispers, then laughs. Then cries. Then howls. The sounds were muffled, but seemed to become clearer and clearer with each passing night.

"Where the heck are those noises coming from?" I asked Stacy one evening.

She blinked herself awake. "Huh?"

"I hear voices. Coming from the walls," I said.

"Oh . . ." she said.

"I'm serious," I said.

"That's not coming from the walls," she said. "It's coming from me."

"From you?"

"From inside me," she said, pulling off the covers and pointing at her crotch.

I snorted at her.

"Listen," she said, pulling my head into her lap and pressing my ear against her vagina.

It was like listening to the ocean in a hairy flesh seashell.

"You're playing!" I said.

She giggled. It was all a joke.

But then I heard it . . .

A voice, inside of her.

I couldn't understand the words. A woman crying, babbling in a deranged language. Then she screamed into my ear and I jumped out from between Stacy's legs.

My girlfriend laughed at me, squinting her dark brown eyes.

"What the hell!" I screamed.

"Told you!" she said.

"What is that?"

"A ghost," she said.

"What!"

"I'm haunted," she said, touching her vagina and smiling.

"How did a ghost get in there?"

"I don't know," she said. "It's been in there for a long time now."

"Why don't you do anything about it?" I asked.

"What can I do?"

"I don't know . . . call a priest?"

"What's a priest going to do? Stick a cross up there and cast the spirits out?"

"Maybe . . ."

"It's really not that big a deal. I've gotten used to it."

"How . . ."

"Actually, I kinda like it."

I frowned at a sailboat on the wall behind her.

"Yeah," she said, spreading her legs across my lap. "Who else has a haunted vagina?" She flattened the bush of pubic hair and spread the lips to examine it. "My other boyfriends thought it was kind of sexy."

I shook my head at her as she smiled. I found it repulsive. But the fact that I was scared of her vagina seemed to turn her on.

She made love to me after that. For her, it was the wildest sex we ever had. She had me pinned down underneath her, sucking on my crusty lower lip, sliding my penis into her ghostly regions and getting off on the terrified look on my face. But for me, it was the most awkward sex I'd ever had. I swear I could feel strange things inside of her that night. Ghostly breaths against the tip of my dick.

But we were madly in love! I didn't even consider leaving her because of her ghost vagina. She meant everything to me. I loved her this >< much! (That means infinitely).

I've been consumed by her ever since the day we met. We were strangers who somehow passed out on a city bus together, my head in her lap, her curly brown hair encasing me like a blanket, hot breath on the back of my neck. When we awoke, she said "That was cozy," and I smiled at her. She was very tall, especially for an Asian girl. Almost a foot taller than me. With silky curled hair and tiny oval glasses.

Then she said she had a snugly bed at her place if we wanted to continue sleeping. I agreed. I thought she wanted to have sex. The whole walk home my eyes were glossy at her, trying to hide my hard-on under my coat. But she really just wanted to sleep. It was late. Both of us worked the swing shift. We went into her studio apartment, the floor covered with laundry that she insisted was all clean, and stripped down to our shirts, underwear and socks. She was right. It was definitely a comfortable bed. It was the biggest, fluffiest bed I've ever been in. She snuggled me like a teddy bear all night. We didn't even know each other's names, but it was one of the nicest moments I've ever spent with another person.

The next morning, we introduced ourselves.

"Steve!" she said, hopping out of bed to the kitchen counter, "I hate that name!"

I could see her cocoa nipples through her t-shirt. She must have taken her bra off sometime during the night.

"Sorry . . ." I said.

"Ha-ha!" she said, eating Lucky Charms out of the box.

"When do you want to do this again?" she asked me.

I shrugged.

"Tonight?" she asked.

I nodded, pulling on my pants.

On the way out the door, she said, "Meet you on the bus."

For three weeks, we slept in the same bed together. We never had sex. We never kissed. We never took off more clothes than our pants. We just dreamed together.

The conversations were brief. We didn't go on any dates. We didn't get to know each other. It was just a sleeping arrangement. To her, I was just a stuffed animal with a heartbeat.

But eventually, we started to talk.

I found out her favorite food was stuffed grape leaves and her favorite films were all Russian. She was born in Thailand but was adopted by a wealthy African American couple before she could walk, and spent most of her life in an upscale suburb outside Los Angeles. She spent ten years at the university here in Portland, getting degrees in every subject she could acquire. She wasn't interested in a career. She just liked learning new things, and her parents paid for everything until she turned thirty. That's when they cut her off and she had to drop out to get a job. Unfortunately, her degrees in Philosophy, History, Russian, Anthropology, Psychology, and Humanities were useless in the job market, so she worked at one of the hipster clothing stores downtown. That's when she decided her real passion in life was fashion design, and she's been saving up her money to go back to school ever since.

"I never went to college," I told her.

"Never ever?" she asked.

"I was busy trying to be a musician. I sang and played guitar. I wanted to be like Beck or the guy from Soul Coughing. But after 10 years of going nowhere, I gave up. Crowds just didn't like me. Night clubs stopped booking me for shows. I kept playing my music at open mic night at Produce Row, but eventually quit. I got sick of the lack of applause. I got sick of people ignoring me, talking at their tables like I wasn't even there. It was just a big waste of time."

"Did playing your music make you happy?" she asked.

"Yes," I said.

"Then it wasn't a waste of time," she said.

That's when I realized I was in love with her.

I didn't realize she was in love with me for months after that. She always said I was cute and small, but that didn't prove anything. A terrier is also cute and small, and I wanted her to love me more than she'd love a terrier.

The day I found out she loved me was the first day we made love. We were walking in the park blocks, down by the art museum, talking about music. She told me she wanted to build a theremin and start a band. I asked if I could be in her band. She said no. She wanted to play Schubert and Debussy on the theremin, and said that I wouldn't fit in. Then we talked about how she planned to give a theremin rendition of Death and the Maiden, and how she wanted to incorporate it into bondage performance.

As we were walking, we passed a grubby homeless man. Probably forty years old, sleeping on a park bench, shivering, wet. I recognized him. His name was Donut. Or at least I've heard his friends address him as Donut. Without thinking, I took off my coat and wrapped it around him. It was odd, because I haven't even given change to the homeless in years. When I first moved to Portland, I used to almost daily. If I had change and somebody asked for it, I would give it to them. But I eventually stopped. Mostly because I stopped using cash and was paying for everything with a debit card. I just didn't have change to give away. But they kept asking. Corner after corner, day after day. When I did have change to give, they wouldn't thank me for it. When I apologized for not having change, they would get pissed off and spit on my shoes. Donut happened to be the worst of them. He was a stocky black guy with a bright orange sweater who strolled around Pioneer Square. He wouldn't ask me for change outright. First, he would ask me if I had a problem with black people. I would say no. He would then ask me for money. Then I would give it to him, as if that was proof that I truly did not have a problem with black people. He would follow me for a block and ask for a little more. I would give him whatever I had, even a dollar or two. Then he'd ask for a little more. If I ever refused him, he would call me a racist.

He'd say, "Oh, I see now, you're a skinhead. Well, sieg heil, skinhead!" He'd continue yelling at me until I was two blocks away. "Sieg Heil! Sieg Heil!"

So, after half a dozen confrontations like that, I avoided all interaction with the homeless. I didn't even make eye contact. But on that day, walking in the park blocks, I gave my $200 coat to Donut, the same homeless guy who called me a racist for not giving him money.

I'm not sure why I did it. I didn't want to give him the coat. I didn't do it because I had something to prove. I just saw a guy freezing on a park bench, covered him with my coat, and continued on. Maybe it was because I was with Stacy. Maybe I was just so happy walking next to her that it made me want to make somebody else happy, too. I don't know.

But after she saw me give away my coat as if it were the most common thing to do in the world, Stacy stopped me in the park, leaned down and kissed me as deeply as she possibly could, and then she told me that she loved me with her shiny dark eyes.

That night, we made love, and the next thing I knew she was moving her big fluffy bed into my place.

Not long after that, I ran into Donut again. He was still calling me a Nazi, wearing my $200 coat over his orange sweater. I couldn't stop smiling at him. He sieg heiled me and I just smiled back. I could tell it just pissed him off even more, because he threatened to beat the crap out of me, but I was just so happy that morning that nothing could possibly bother me.

CHAPTER TWO

I haven't had sex with Stacy for over a month now, but I'm still crazy for her. I still love everything about her. Her smell, her smile, the sound of her voice. She has unique ways of doing things that are so cute I want to cry.

Like, this is the way she eats a burger from Carl's Jr:

First, she'll wipe off all of the mustard, mayonnaise and ketchup with a plastic butter knife and swirl it into a puddle on the burger's wrapper. Then she'll disassemble the burger and cut the buns into small squares. She'll stab a piece of bun with a fork, then stab one other ingredient. Either a chunk of meat, some cheese, a pickle, a tomato, or lettuce. Then she'll swirl the food in the sauce and eat it.

"I like my food separated," she always says. "I like to control the flavor."

She does that with all her food. Pizza, burritos, sandwiches, lasagna, even curry stews. It's incredibly cute. I also have a quirky way of eating. Whenever I take a bite of food, I never let my lips touch the eating utensil. I just use my teeth. Stacy doesn't think it's cute, though. She hates the sound of my teeth scraping against a metal fork. She always tells me to stop. I don't stop, though, because she's even cuter when she's annoyed.

Other cute things about her:

She pets every animal she ever sees in public. She dances naked to Prince. She licks her glasses clean before she reads. She adores public transportation and gets excited whenever she sees a bus stop, or the light rail. She gives tips to everyone including cooks, bus drivers, fast food employees, and flight attendants, whether they are allowed to accept tips or not. Though she usually tips pretty low. She calls water pouring from faucets waterfalls. She collects doll houses. She plays with her eyelashes. She loves goldfish and likes to stare at them in their bowls making fish-faces at them, mimicking them when they open and close their mouths at her as if to communicate.

The only thing that kind of annoys me is that she tends to order steak at seafood restaurants, lobster at steak houses, burgers at Mexican restaurants, fajitas at burger joints, sushi at Chinese restaurants, chow mein at Japanese restaurants, and hot dogs whenever they are available on a menu at any restaurant. Especially when she drags me out to eat German food, which I hate, and then orders a chicken caesar salad and clam chowder.

She does the same thing to me with Russian food, but she has so much fun talking to the employees in Russian that I completely enjoy myself, even when I have to eat beet salad and ham pickle soup.

She's the best person in the world to be around when she's happy.

CHAPTER THREE

After a while, not having sex has taken its toll on our relationship.

"I don't see what the big deal is," she says.

"I'm just not comfortable with it," I say.

I tell her we can do other things. Both of us are interested in giving anal sex, but neither of us are interested in receiving it. She's tried her strap-on with me before and it was far from pleasurable. I'm not going to do that again.

Same goes with oral sex. We both like to receive it, but neither of us want to give it. Normally we can compromise on oral. If I give it to her, she will give it to me. Unfortunately, I'm not willing to go near her vagina anymore. Not with my penis, not with my tongue.

"It's not like you have to stick your tongue inside of me," she says. "You can just lick my glowworm."

Glowworm is her pet name for a clitoris.

"It's on the outside," she says.

"But still . . ." I say.

"I'll keep my legs closed," she says. "You won't even hear it."

I don't reply. She turns away from me and takes off her work clothes, as if I agreed. Folding her glasses and putting them back in their case. Her movements are cold and mechanical. She must be pissed. Giving me the silent treatment like the time I washed her white fuzzy coat wrong, or the time she found pictures of my old girlfriends and I wouldn't let her throw them out. On those occasions, she ignored me and locked herself in the bedroom. On this occasion, however, she wants to get intimate. She won't look me in the eyes as she unbuttons my shirt and pulls off my pants.

She picks me up and turns me upside-down, then plops us on the bed. I don't know how she's able to lift me. She's much taller than me and weighs a bit more, but she's not muscular. She's soft and slender. Both of us are.

In sixty-nine position, it's a bit awkward. I'm on top this time and her legs are closed. My tongue scratches against wiry black pubic hair while searching for her glowworm. I feel a bit safe with her thighs pressed together tightly, but my tongue has to dig between them to find the right spot. Stacy kisses the backs of my thighs. Because of my height, her mouth can't really reach my penis while I'm on top. But she kisses my legs and licks my ass.

"It's not working," I say, as she nibbles on my scrotum.

She lifts my ass and twists her neck until she can get beneath me and take my penis into her mouth. I mostly just feel teeth. A bad angle. Her front teeth dig into the skin, killing any sort of erection I almost had. Her legs part slightly. I'm able to find her clit and twirl my tongue around it. She's more wet then I expected. Must be horny as hell. I don't have to do much. She hasn't had sex for so long that riding a bicycle would probably give her an orgasm.

She groans around my penis. I look back to see she's making a fish face at me. Fish lips around my dick like she would make while looking in the goldfish bowl. I don't know if she's trying to be sexy with that face or what, but for some reason it gives me a full erection. Maybe it's just exciting to see her beautiful tan lips wrapped around me.

I go back to the glowworm and suck it into my mouth,

slurping it and the skin around it as deep into my mouth as it will stretch. Then I release it, then suck it in again. I do that to the rhythm of her blow job. And inside of my mouth, I tickle it with my tongue and the glowworm dances happily between my lips.

Stacy spreads her legs a little more. I don't know if it is on purpose or by accident. I can see the crack of her vagina completely now, staring up at me as I lick.

There's a rumbling inside of it. Like a mild earthquake in the distance. The lips spread and a voice calls out to me. I lick Stacy as fast as I can, trying to get her to orgasm quickly so I can get away from her vagina. The voice grows louder. I struggle on top of her, but Stacy grips me by the waist so that I can't go anywhere and takes me deeper into her mouth.

I close my eyes. Forget the sights and sounds, just concentrate on the feelings. Concentrate on my flesh inside of Stacy's mouth. Concentrate on her flesh inside of my mouth. I'm getting close to orgasm. Stacy is too. I let my worries slide completely as she squeezes her thighs tightly together, preparing to cum.

Something bumps inside her. Something pushes at my chin and knocks the glowworm out of my lips. Pissed off, Stacy slaps the side of my ass as hard as she can. I continue. Her belly pushes against me, like there's something moving in her womb. The flesh balloons outward. I try to ignore it. Stacy's doing something perfectly with her mouth. I don't feel her teeth at all and she's able to take me all the way down. There's no way I'm going to stop her.

Her belly expands, lifting me up several inches. I think Stacy realizes something odd is going on, too, but she can't stop either. She feels nine months pregnant now. Her skin stretching to its limit. No, it keeps stretching. She's getting almost twice as pregnant. Stacy orgasms and jerks her head back, cries out against my asshole. Then she puts me back in her mouth and whines as she sucks. Something is moving inside of her. I'm shifted side to side, but I'm so close. So close . . .

I explode into her mouth as a hand explodes out of the vagina. I shriek and jump backward, landing on top of Stacy's head. My penis shoved completely down her throat, cumming inside her. She gags, choking, and shoves me off.

I hit the floor. Stacy coughs my cum out of her lungs. I look up at her as she coughs, mouth wide open, unable to say a word. She stands and examines her belly as it shuffles. It moves about like it's filled with a million cockroaches. And between her legs, a skeletal hand is reaching out of her.

"What the fuck!" finally comes out of me, as I crawl away.

Stacy just watches her body in amazement as the hand clutches onto her leg and pulls. Another hand emerges and grabs her other thigh, trying to pull itself out of there.

Then it dawns on her. Yes, Stacy, this is actually happening to you. She looks at me with wide dilated pupils, frightened of her own vagina.

"Help . . ." she says. Her voice a soft croak.

I leap to my feet and grab the skeletal hands away from her thighs. I have no idea what I think I'm doing. I pull on the skeletal arms and a skull pops out at me. Animated, chattering its teeth. Stacy grabs onto the bed frame and I pull as hard as I can, ripping the skeleton halfway out.

It throws me back, thrashes at Stacy and knocks her to

the floor. I watch as the skeletal figure, waist deep inside of my girlfriend, claws at the hardwood floor, crawling out from between her legs.

Stacy is crying in a panic now. Her face bright red, her mouth drooling wide open, her eyes so squinty wet that she can't see anything anymore.

"Do something!" she cries.

But I don't know what to do.

I pick up a turtle-shaped lamp and hit the skeleton with it. The turtle's head pops off. I hit harder, then harder, until I find the right angle to break its skull.

I cut my hand on the shattered lamp. Blood spills onto the corpse. It's still moving.

Flesh begins to grow on its bones like moss, lightning-fast. The lamp is in little pieces, and my blood is leaking everywhere. Stacy screams in Russian at me, angry profanities that I don't understand.

I step away from the corpse. It is growing organs. Blood red balls fill the eye sockets of the skull, and the skeleton looks up at me. It releases a deep moan. I run to the corner of the room and pick up the night stand, knocking clocks, glasses, a jar of coins all over the floor. The skull watches me, cries at me, as I lower the night stand onto its neck. Then I drop all of my weight on top of it.

A loud crack. It stops moving. It stops moaning. I turn over the night stand. Its spinal cord has been severed. Its head crushed. Blue ink dribbles out of its mouth.

Stacy whines, shrieking at the corpse still halfway inside her. Her hands twitch inches away from it, wanting it out of her but she doesn't want to touch it.

I pull on the corpse, but it pulls Stacy with it. She cries. I pull again. She just moves again.

"Hold on to the leg of the bed," I say, in the calmest possible voice.

She's hiccupping now, leaning back to hold onto the bed.

She doesn't watch as I pull it out of her. With each tug she cries out. I cry as well, with my sliced-open hand rubbing against the thing's rib cage. Once it slips all the way out, she leaps to her feet and runs out of the room.

I look down at the body. It seems to be melting. Its flesh turns to blue, red, and orange mucus. Its bones melting into egg whites, crumbling into baking soda. I drape the big fluffy blanket over its body and leave the room.

CHAPTER FOUR

Stacy is standing in the corner of the living room, behind the couch, covering herself with the curtain. She doesn't realize that the people walking on the sidewalk outside can see her nude backside.

"Let's go for a drink," I tell her.

She nods her head and goes for her purse, digging through its contents, not looking for anything in particular. I get us some pants and t-shirts from the hamper in the laundry room.

"Here," I say.

She sniffles and puts her purse down, then gets dressed. Strangely, she's come out of it unscathed. My hand is still bleeding everywhere. I can't feel much pain. Must be in shock. But her stomach has flattened back to normal. No stretch marks, no tearing of her vagina, no blood. Some claw marks are on her inner thighs, but they are just white scratches. The claws just barely broke the skin.

I bandage up my wound and put on the smelly crusty clothes. We go into the garage and slip on some junky old tennis shoes that we were planning to give to Goodwill.

"Ready?" I ask, wiping away her tears.

She doesn't hear me, busy examining a spider web that has recently formed inside the doorway of one of her old doll houses.

We go out to the Kennedy School across town. It's an old elementary school that was bought by a brewing company. All of the classrooms have been turned into bars, restaurants, tobacco lounges, and hotel rooms. Stacy's not a big fan of all the breweries in Portland. She just doesn't like beer at all. She prefers drinking cocktails in the Pearl District. But I love breweries. And I need a very strong brewery beer right now. I'm also thinking if she's not in a condition to go back home tonight, we can just stay in one of the school's guest rooms.

She doesn't speak to me for a couple hours. In the Cypress Room at Kennedy School, I feed her screwdrivers with freshly squeezed orange juice and I drink the Sunflower IPA.

I try to ask her questions, try to learn more about how the heck a man-sized creature could crawl out of her vagina, where the heck that thing came from, and how long has this all been going on. But she doesn't know.

She tells me everything that has to do with her haunted insides. She tells me that ever since she was a little kid she's heard noises coming from inside her. She thought it was normal. Her parents never noticed. Or pretended not to notice. When she was six years old, for a few months, she had an imaginary friend who used to come out of her vagina to play with her. Another little girl, about her age, with paper white skin and funny slimy horns on her head. She doesn't remember much from that time, but had always assumed the girl was just her imagination. She thought maybe it was just her young mind giving a form to the voices she heard coming from inside of her. Now she is not so sure.

When she was a sophomore in high school, she realized that her vagina was different from other girls' vaginas. Her first love was a girl named Charlee, who was a nerdy freshman who always spoke in a fake French accent. The first time they were naked together, giggling and scared, Stacy's vagina called out to Charlee and knocked the French accent right out of her voice.

"That's fucked up," the girl said.

Stacy didn't understand. She tried to get close to Charlee but she pushed her back.

"Don't touch me," the girl said, and they never spoke to each other ever again.

She stayed away from girls after that, made friends with guys. But most high school guys always wanted to get into her pants, so she only hung out with the dungeons and dragons skater kids who were nice and somewhat fun, but most importantly they were way too shy to solicit sex from her.

In college, she ended up getting drunk and sleeping with some wannabe Beat poet English major. She warned him about having a haunted vagina, but that only turned him on. After they screwed, he said that it was the most amazing thing he'd ever done. They dated for a while, and he worshiped her vagina. He told all of his friends about her and would even have them listen to the voices through her pants. All of them thought she was brilliant. She brought magic into their worlds. She was proof that their drunken philosophical discussions of rebellion against reality were somewhat correct. And when she got bored of her boyfriend, she moved on to one of his friends. And when she got bored with him, she would move on to another. All of them treated her like a goddess.

She stayed in college until she was thirty, becoming something of a legend on campus. Near the end of her college years, she started going to goth parties and charging money to all the little goth boys and girls nearly 8 to 10 years younger than her for the chance to listen to her vagina for a few minutes. There would be lines out the door to see her. Eventually, a rumor went around that it was all fake. She just had some kind of wireless speaker inside of her playing tape-recorded noises. Nobody believed her after that. She was no longer dating any of the college kids, since they were all so young, so there was no one who had gotten intimate enough with her to back up her story. And she didn't really care to prove it to them. A few guys still paid to listen to her vagina, but once she realized they were just doing it to rub the sides of their heads between her legs, she stopped doing it completely.

That's all the information she had for me. It all seemed harmless to her, before. Just something that made her unique and special. She's never been scared of it. She might have been scared that people would find out about it as a teenager, but she was never scared of what might be lurking inside of her.

She drinks screwdriver after screwdriver until she can barely walk.

CHAPTER FIVE

We're drunkenly relaxed, wandering through the halls of the school/brewery, staring at all the murals of scary dancing children with the faces of eighty-year-olds. I go to the front desk and get us a room.

"We're going to stay here tonight," I tell Stacy.

She sways at me, leaning her head back with her eyes closed and a dumb smile on her face. I get a pitcher of Hammerhead from the movie theater, which used to be the school's auditorium, and take my giant drunken girlfriend into the room.

I continue drinking, fidgeting with my hand wound that has finally stopped bleeding and is beginning to itch, sitting in a chair next to the chalkboard. The room was once a classroom. They left the chalkboards on the walls. Employees have drawn flowers on the board in red and yellow chalk, with the words "Welcome to Kennedy School" written in girly cursive. Stacy sits on the edge of the bed next to me and tries some of my beer, then spits it back into the glass.

"Yuck," she says. "I wanted the raspberry beer."

"You didn't say you wanted anything," I tell her.

"I want the raspberry."

"You want me to get you some?"

She nods her head sloppily against her shoulder.

"Okay, I'll get another pitcher."

I decide to just get her a 22 ounce bottle of Ruby at the front desk, rather than a pitcher.

The school has gotten pretty quiet. The restaurant is closed. It's just a few minutes before beer-o'clock. Looking at the old pictures on the walls of the school when it first opened decades ago, little monochrome children kneeling in the dirt, holding their school projects. A few of those same school projects are a few feet away, behind glass: crudely painted bird houses. I wonder about all of those kids. Most of them must be dead now. Their bird houses like ghosts they left behind.

I get back to the room.

"Steve . . ." Stacy calls out as I open the door.

I turn the corner. Her pants are off and she's probing her vagina with her arm, almost all the way up to her elbow.

"What are you doing?" I ask.

She laughs at me.

"Look," she says, pulling her vaginal lips open. They are stretchy like rubber.

Then she laughs, hysterically. I chuckle too in a nervous kind of way.

"I didn't know it could do that before!" She lets the lips go and they slap back into place. Her head wobbles at me. She's way too drunk. I hide her beer behind the bed.

I take her hands away from her vagina, and try to put her pants back on.

"No," she says, kicking her pants away.

"Stacy!"

She laughs at me. I keep trying to put her pants back on but she just kicks and laughs. Then she sits up and looks at me.

"I want you to look inside," she says.

I snicker, like it was a joke.

"I can't see for myself," she says. "I want you to tell me what it looks like in there. If you can see ghosts."

I look up at her cute brown eyes and can't tell her no.

She leans back on the bed and stretches out her vagina lips again. The hole is big enough to fit a football through. I bend down and look inside.

"See anything?" she asks.

"No," I say. Just a fleshy cavity.

Stacy spreads her lips out farther. I help her, pushing the labia apart, peering in. The hole might be wide at the opening, but it shrinks to the size of a pea only inches within. I dig my hand inside, but my hands are dry and abrasive.

"Ow," she says.

She builds spit in her mouth and then rubs it inside of her as a quick lubricant. I slide my hands in, both of them, and spread the flesh apart as wide as I can. It stretches to about basketball width. I look within. There's a pin of light deep inside of her. Maybe a reflection of the lamp against a pool of moisture? No. It's some kind of light.

"What do you think it is?" I ask.

"Maybe it's the ghost," she says.

"No, I don't think so. It's just some kind of light."

Stacy lets go of her labia and retrieves the beer that I had hidden from her. She cracks it open against the edge of the table and takes a chug. I drink a pint from my pitcher. We sip our drinks in silence for a while. The more Stacy drinks, the more sober she seems to become. The more I drink, the more retarded I become.

"I want you to go in there," Stacy tells me, calmer than she has been all night.

I don't know what she means at first, my mind lost in a game of solitaire.

"I can't just forget about this and get on with the rest of my life," she says. "I've got to find out what's going on in there."

"What do you want me to do about it?"

"That skeleton thing was almost bigger than you," she says. "If it could fit through then you can fit."

"What!"

"I think my vagina is a gateway of some kind. That light you saw must be the light at the end of the tunnel. The entrance to another world."

"I'm not going in there!"

I laugh at her.

"Steve," she says, holding my knee. "You have to. I can't possibly figure out what's going on without your help."

I chug the last of my beer, snickering. There's no way I'm agreeing to that.

"If you love me," she says. "You'll do it."

She's completely serious.

She's looking at me like this is the ultimate test of our love. If I don't do it she will leave me for somebody who will.

My voice is shaky. "I can't."

"Please!" she says, angry-faced at me, gripping my knee as if to hurt me.

I stand up and go to the bathroom.

She follows.

"All you have to do is crawl to the end of the tunnel and look out," she says to me while I'm urinating. "Then come right back and tell me what you see. Nothing will happen to you, I promise."

"Just as far as the light?" I ask.

"Yes!" she nearly screams the reply at me.

I finish pissing and flush the toilet.

"I'll give it a try," I tell her. "For you."

She closes her eyes and nods her head at me.

Stacy tries taking off my shirt.

"What are you doing?" I ask.

"You'll go in easier without your clothes on."

I shake my head at her, but allow her to remove my clothes. For some reason, she takes off all of her clothes, too.

"This isn't going to work," I say. "That thing was supernatural. I'm not."

"We'll make it work," she says.

"What if I suffocate? What if you stop being stretchy once I'm in there?"

"Shhhh!" she says, leading me to the bed. "It's going to work. You'll see."

She climbs onto the bed and lies on her back. Staring at me with her cold dark eyes, she spreads her legs like she wants me to fuck her. Then she masturbates.

"Do you think this is hot or something?" I ask.

She bites her lip. "I need to moisten up."

I laugh out loud. I'm so drunk that I actually believe this is going to happen.

Then she pulls her lips apart as wide as she can, about fourteen inches. Her hips pop out of joint like the jaws of a snake opening up for its prey.

"Come on," she says.

She's so wet that she can't hold onto the sides very well. They keep slipping out of her fingers. I crawl onto the bed in front of her and kiss her, she tongues my cheek sloppily. I make a fin with my hand and slide that in first, then my other hand, and separate her opening as wide as I can.

I look up at her. She doesn't say anything. Just licks her trembling lips. I notice that I'm also trembling. My hands shaking like the first time I ever had sex.

"If I get claustrophobic I'm coming back out," I tell her.

She pushes my face down into her crotch, like she does when she wants oral sex. I push my arms through up to the elbows. I can see them moving inside of her belly. Then I put the top of my head into the opening and push.

Stacy cries out and begins masturbating again, I can feel her fingers against the back of my head. I don't know if it turns her on or if my scratchy hair is hurting her and she needs more lubrication. I push again. She cries out again. It's impossible. I'm stuck. I shove again, but don't budge an inch.

I pull out.

"What!" Stacy says.

"It's not working," I say.

"Yes it will," she says.

"There's no way," I tell her.
"It's going to happen whether you like it or not."

She's not giving up for anything.

She takes scissors out of her purse, the ones she uses as a toenail clipper, and cuts off all my hair. The dull blades mixed with her furious movements make it a painful fucking experience even with all the alcohol in my system. Then she shaves it down smooth with a disposable pink razor. I think I'm beginning to feel hungover. She greases up my entire body with some girly skin stuff, lotion or oil or something. It mostly absorbs into my skin, but I do feel sufficiently lubed.

"This time it's going to work," she says to me, kissing my bald head.

She lubes up her vagina as well.

"Push as hard as you can this time," she says. "Plunge into me. Don't worry, it won't hurt."

I don't care about it hurting. I'm more worried about suffocating . . . or what is waiting for me within. At least there haven't been any noises coming out of there.

She positions us on the bed, and shoves my head into her crotch again. This time she pushes into me as I push into her. Arms first, they slide in very easily. The top of my head also goes in with ease—it still makes her cry out, makes her masturbate—but I doubt I'll get much farther than this.

I push a little, move an inch. Push again, move an inch. My nose is practically in her asshole now. I hesitate to go in any farther. There's no way I can breathe in there. The corpse that came out of her was undead. It didn't need to breathe.

Stacy can tell I'm not trying anymore. I can sense her anger building. She smacks at my arms in her belly in a *come on, come on* kind of way.

I try to pull out again, but Stacy lunges at me. She stands up and squats over me, dropping all of her weight down on top of me, and I find myself sliding up into her abysmal cavity until I'm up to my chest, her vaginal lips closing tight around my armpits. She squats down on me again, harder, until I'm in up to my belly.

Holy crap . . . This is really happening. I'm really going all the way inside of her . . .

My face pressed against wet flesh. My eyes closed. I can breathe, but just barely. My face is hot with my breath. Stacy screams out and plops onto her back again, masturbating furiously against my lower spine. I position my head face-forward and try to open my eyes but the vaginal juices burn them. I can hear Stacy's muffled whines on the other side of the flesh. I can feel her grabbing her breasts against the back of my shoulders, I can feel her holding me inside of her belly as a way to comfort me one last time before my voyage.

I push off with my feet. It seems looser the farther in I get. After a few inches, I feel Stacy's hands grab my ass and shove me from behind. I straighten out as my buttocks go through, now lying inside of her. She grabs my legs and jostles them in, using my ankles as handles. I squirm forward.

The next thing I know, her lips close up around my wriggling toes.

CHAPTER SIX

It dawns on me. I'm all the way inside of her. I'm like a human penis.

That thought actually gives me an erection. The fleshy walls around me begin rumbling. I can hear Stacy outside masturbating in a rage. Her flesh shivers, sweats, all around me.

I wriggle forward and the walls quake in reaction to my movement. After a couple feet of wriggling, the cave opens up a bit. It's still tight around me, but I'm able to use my legs to kick off. The cave quakes harder. I open my eyes. The light is up ahead. I move toward it. Soon the vaginal tunnel loosens up enough for me to get on my hands and knees so I can crawl through, but I have to push the meat ceiling up with the back of my head as I go. This seems to drive Stacy crazy.

I crawl for maybe twenty feet. The tunnel has gotten so loose that I could probably stand up and walk in a hunched over kind of way, but I probably wouldn't be able to keep my balance on the flabby ground. I'm so far away from the entrance that I shouldn't possibly be able to feel Stacy's masturbating anymore, but I still do, rumbling all around me. I still can hear her moaning through the skin. I can't tell how far away I am from the light. Could be halfway there. Could be a mile away.

No, I see it. It's right there. Not ten feet in front of me. A hole. A very small hole.

The cave gets smaller the closer I get to the opening. Maybe it leads to another vagina. Maybe this is a tunnel between dimensions, connected by two women's vaginas. Perhaps I will arrive in this world as a skeleton and will scare the hell out of some poor woman as I crawl out of her. Maybe the skeleton that came out of Stacy was this girl's boyfriend.

I shove myself toward the hole and stick a finger through the opening. The walls shudder all around me. I just need to peek through and then I can turn around and go back.

I get up to the opening and peer through with one eye. Nothing, just light. I put my hands through and pull back the sides.

A sky.

I stick my head out, and the sides slip out of my hands, wrap around my neck in a comforting choke . . .

I look down.

I'm sticking out on the edge of some kind of cliff. About fifteen or twenty feet off the ground. Stacy was right. Her vagina is some kind of gateway to another dimension. The sky is cloudy and purplish. No sun at all. Other than that, I see green grass, a forest, and an old rotten wooden fence. But that's all I can see.

Time to turn back. The walls are trembling around me. The cliff is also trembling. The trees and grass begin shuffling like it's an earthquake.

The walls squeeze tight around me. Stacy's having an orgasm. I hear her voice in the wind, moaning, as the walls get tighter and tighter. Then fluids flow from the flesh around me and the cave squeezes me out, spitting me into the world below.

CHAPTER SEVEN

I wake up. Spit blood and soil out of my mouth. Thunder is in the clouds.

I look up. The cliff goes up as high as I can see, into the clouds. I can't see the opening up there, but I can guess it's near the black rocks that have been darkened by moisture. Not too high up, but I was much higher than I thought I was. My head is pounding at me. A large lump is growing on the side of my bald scalp. It's squid-shaped and a bit blubbery.

I try to climb up the cliff-side, but the surface is too sheer. My feet can't get any foot holds. I get three feet off the ground and slip, cutting my toes on the way down and twisting my left ankle a bit.

This is seriously fucked. I look around. Where the hell am I?

The face of the cliff is covered in dozens of claw marks. Must have been that skeletal creature. I examine the forest. There could be more of them around here. There is an old fence buried in mud and rot, indicating some kind of civilization is nearby or had been nearby at one time.

I continue my effort to climb the wall. No luck. My feet are scraped, bruised, bloodied, and I think I've seriously injured my big toe. What the fuck am I going to do?

The wind bites my naked back. I curl into a ball to protect myself from the cold, shivering and growing gooseflesh. A woman's voice is carried on the wind, crying out some unintelligible words. I leap off of the ground and climb the cliff furiously, but slip and my belly is scraped against the side of the cliff as I fall back down.

The voice continues, only softer. It sounds like she's arguing with somebody. But I don't understand the words.

I've got to find something that will help me climb out of here. Maybe I can make a ladder out of the fence.

I try to get the wood out of the ground but the wood folds into halves when I pull on it. It's about as sturdy as wet cardboard. I go to another side of the fence and push on the wood. It breaks in my hands. It's been devoured by termites and is soggy in the middle.

Maybe there's a fallen log in the forest . . .

I step carefully into the woods, making sure I don't step on any sharp rocks, making sure nothing jumps out at me. Looking back every five seconds to ensure I don't lose sight of the opening in the cliff.

The forest is silent. The only sound is my breath, my feet hitting the ground, and the wind in the leaves.

The voice on the wind comes and goes. Sometimes I can almost make out a word or two, but can't comprehend what it's saying. It might be somebody who can help me, somebody human. But I'd rather not run into anyone here. Who knows what kind of weird creatures live inside of Stacy's vagina . . .

The wind dies down. The voice gone. There's some kind of building up ahead. A triangle of red peeking out of the trees. I approach it slowly, taking time between steps to listen to what might be lurking in the forest.

It's an old log cabin. I step out of the woods into a clearing, an acre of land where the trees have been cut down to stumps. I cover my privates as I tiptoe toward the side of the building. It's very quiet. No sign of life, not even birds in the air. I look in through a window, but it's dark inside. Walking around to the front, I stare across the clearing. The distance is just forest. There are no roads or trails leading up to the cabin. There's no real sign that anybody has ever lived here.

I go to the door. Knock twice.

"Hello?"

No response. I feel stupid for asking, but feel better that I did. Inside, it is mostly dark. There is a hairball of light coming in from the windows but it doesn't brighten much. I wait for my eyes to adjust.

It is musty. The floor is covered in dust. Actually, it looks more like ash than dust, almost an inch deep. It sticks to the bottom of my heels as I cross the room. The furniture is wooden and poorly crafted, like it was built by a sloppy pioneer. The cabin seems to have been made for a single person. There is a single chair, a small table, and a crooked bed with blue moldy sheets. On a shelf, there are old dolls. A dozen of them, hiding behind cobwebs.

I look through a chest for some clothes. There are several strips of cloth, more like rags. At the bottom, I find a pair of overalls. They are as hard as rawhide, but I put them on. Kind of large for me, and gritty against my privates, but it'll keep out the cold. I also find some boots under the bed. Caked with mud on the inside and out, but they're better than walking barefoot. I might even be able to climb that cliff with these.

There's nothing else of use here. Except, maybe . . .

A weapon.

There's a rifle on the wall. I pick it up, examine it. Rusted. Even if I had bullets for it the thing would probably explode in my face if I tried to fire it. There's a knife on the wooden table. It'll have to do.

On the way out, I see some movement glistening through the cracked window. There's a figure walking across the clearing past the cabin. Human, I think. I hide behind the wall and peek only one eye out of the window to watch it.

It's not exactly human. Its skin is white and red. A female, walking nude, casually through the grass. Some kind of weird bunny ears sticking out of her head. She doesn't make a sound, just passes the cabin and disappears into the woods.She leaves behind a floral scent that tickles my nostrils as if I've just inhaled a swarm of tiny fluttering moths. It's not like perfume. More like flower sweat.

I wait a few minutes. Then leave the cabin. I try looking through the forest to see where the girl came from, where she went to. But there aren't any houses that I can see.

There is a shed behind the cabin. I go to that. It is filled with old mud-caked tools, including an axe.

That's what I need. I drop the knife and take the axe. It's old but still strong enough to fend off attackers. In the back of the shed, there's a ladder. Exactly what I needed. I pull it out, but the wood is soft. Two of the rungs pop off before I get it out of the shed. I'm not going to be able to climb the cliff with this. Even on the top rung, if it could hold me, I'd still need to climb five feet before I could reach the opening.

It's worth a try.

I run through the woods as fast as I can, hoping the ladder doesn't break apart on me. Carrying the axe at the same time makes it awkward, but I'm not dropping my weapon. The ladder falls to pieces once I get to the side of the cliff. But I bend down, pick up the pieces, and reassemble it. Then lean it against the edge of the cliff and give it a try.

It almost works. A few of the rungs are sturdy enough to hold my weight, but the rest just break off when I step on them. I try climbing without the ladder, but just rip open the wound on my hand.

The axe . . .

I climb the ladder as far as I can safely, then strike the cliff with the axe. I put all my weight on the axe and put very little weight on the weak rungs. Then I pull the axe out and strike again, higher, and continue up.

I can see the opening now. Well, not the opening, but I can see where the earth turns to flesh up there. That's where the hole is. At the top rung, the ladder breaks into halves. Some rungs on one half, some rungs on the other, many of them just dropping to the ground. But I'm supported by the axe, for now, balancing. I'm not too far from the fleshy part. I might be able to drop the ladder and climb it on my own.

Balancing the ladder just right, so it can hold me up for just one moment more. I pull the axe out of the cliff and strike higher. Blood gushes through the rock and onto my legs. One foot slips and the ladder drops, but I'm still hanging onto the axe handle. I find some footholds in the rock and climb the last few feet, using the axe as support. The blood oozes slowly. It doesn't effect my climb, but has an intense copper stink.

My hand reaches the hole and I force myself inside. Moisture or no moisture, I shove myself within, leaving the axe in the side of the cliff.

CHAPTER EIGHT

It's tough moving through the fleshy tunnel in the overalls toward Stacy's vagina. I don't see the light ahead, so I move blindly through the meat. It gets moist, but I'm still not able to slide through.

About twenty feet in, I start to hear Stacy's screams ahead of me, her voice vibrates all around my body. I keep pushing. The tunnel bends down. I can feel gravity pulling me forward. When I get to the opening, Stacy is nearly shrieking. I stick my finger out first and hit a denim wall. She's wearing her pants. I stretch my head forward until my mouth is sticking out of her vagina, into her pants. She's not wearing any underwear. The zipper is cold against my lips.

She screams and slaps at me through her pants. I don't recognize her screams. Maybe it's not Stacy. Maybe I've somehow come out of somebody else's vagina.

"Stacy!" I cry through her jeans, trying to suck air through the fabric.

"Wait!" she says. "Don't come out!"

"What's going on?" I say.

"Don't come out!" she says.

Then I realize she's in the middle of driving a car. I can hear the traffic. I can feel the vibration of the engine.

"Pull over and let me out," I tell her.

"No," she says. "We're almost home."

I can hear her breathing heavily. Her muscles are squeezed around my body like she's doing Kegel exercises. The air in her crotch is thick with her vaginal musk.

Strange how much stronger the smell is on the outside than on the inside. I close my eyes and try to relax. My body all cut up and sore. My head swollen and bruised. My hangover now hitting me at full strength. All I want to do is sleep.

Stacy parks and gets out of the car, walking bowlegged up the sidewalk, holding one hand around her humongous pregnant belly, and pushing my head back into her crotch with the other.

When she gets into the house, she unzips her pants and I'm able to breathe fresh air. The morning sun comes in and blinds my eyes.

"Are you okay in there?" she asks.

I see her hair draped down over the opening, like she's trying to peek inside to see me.

"No," I tell her.

I watch the floor as she walks to the couch, pulls off her pants and sits down. She screams as I crawl out of her, probably going to give her some kind of infection with these dirty overalls trailing mud and grit inside of her.

Once I'm halfway out, I push off on the edge of the couch and land face-first on the hardwood floor. She pulls away from me until my legs and feet slip out.

I look back at her and she's holding her crotch, writhing in pain.

"You okay?" I ask.

When I get closer, she wraps her arms around me and kisses me.

"I thought you were gone!" she says.

Her eyes teary at me. "I waited forever."

"I'm sorry," I say.

She looks at the boots and overalls I'm wearing. "Where did this come from?"

"From inside of there."

"It fucking hurt," she says, punching me softly in the chest.

After getting out of the grubby overalls and showering off Stacy's dried juices from my entire body, we sit at the dining room table, drinking coffee, and I tell her everything that happened to me. Her eyes go wild as I speak.

"There's a whole world inside me," she says. Proud of herself.

"Well," I say, "the world isn't really inside of you, but the doorway to the other world is inside of you."

"No, you don't understand," she says. "The world really is in me. It's just really small."

She nods her head with a big smile.

"Why do you say that?" I ask.

"When you went inside of me, I could feel you in there. I could see you through my skin."

"And . . ."

"And you were getting smaller," she says. "The deeper in you went, the smaller you became. I saw your head moving against the inside of my belly, at first it was regular-sized but as you moved deeper in it shrunk to the size of a barbie doll head. Then it was so small I couldn't see it anymore. But I could feel you in me. I could feel you getting smaller and smaller inside of me, the farther in you went. Until I couldn't feel you anymore. I think by that time you were microscopic."

"Maybe . . ." I say.

"The whole world must be some kind of tumor the size of a pea," she says, "hiding somewhere in my womb."

"So I was really just inside of you this whole time?"

"Uh-huh," she says, smiling.

"That girl you saw," Stacy said, eating a piece of cinnamon toast, "did she have slimy horns?"

"I don't know," I say. "It looked like she had bunny ears."

"Maybe she was my imaginary friend from when I was a kid," she says. "All grown up."

"I didn't get a good look at her," I say.

"I wish I could remember her name . . ." Stacy says. "My memories of her seem more like a dream. I don't remember it hurting when she came in and out of my vagina. She was more like a genie coming out of a bottle."

"A ghost?"

"Yeah," she says. "She must be the ghost that I hear inside of me."

"She did move a little funny," I say. "But she didn't look like a ghost."

"Who knows what ghosts look like . . ." Stacy says.

The skeleton has turned to a thick film on our bedroom floor.

"You ruined my blanket," she says to me, bundling up the fluffy blanket stained with skeleton juice.

I don't apologize. "Why do you think it melted like that?"

"Who knows," she says. "Maybe it just wasn't suitable for this world."

"It looked like it was doing fine before I smashed its head," I say.

"Maybe that's just the way people from the womb world die," she says.

We watch the puddle of corpse for a while.

"Are you going to call in sick today?" I ask.

"No," she says. "Can't."

"Let's get some sleep then," I say.

Luckily neither of us have to go into work until the afternoon.

We curl up in bed together, without a blanket. She wraps me in her arms like a teddy bear, the way she always does, and falls asleep against my forehead. My hand is squished against her belly, probably pressing into the clouds of the tiny world inside of her.

CHAPTER NINE

Stacy's gone before I wake up.

We didn't set the alarm. I already missed the bus.

Downtown, Donut really lays into me for my freshly shaved head.

"I'm part Jewish," I tell him.

"So was Adolf Hitler!" he says.

I give him the rest of my Honkin' Huge Burrito so he'll leave me alone. Too sore, too hungover, too late to mess around.

When I get to the call center, sit down at my computer station as if I'm perfectly on time rather than two hours late, I realize that I really shouldn't have bothered coming in today. I still reek of sex, even after showering. My head is pounding. I look like I've gotten into a fight.

"You look horrible," Chaz says to me, his pants pulled above his belly button.

He's the insanely hyperactive portly guy who always invites me to karaoke parties.

"Yeah," I tell him.

"Looks like you've been skateboarding," he says. "I was a pretty good skateboarder in junior high. We should go skateboarding sometime."

"Sure," I tell him.

He just stands there smiling at me, shifting his weight from side to side. I ignore him, turn on my computer and log into the queue. I can hardly move my fingers. They are swollen. Dirt crammed under my fingernails. The large scab in my palm making it difficult to close my hand. My fingers are very pale, except for the fingertips which are dark red for some reason, like I've cut off the circulation at my knuckles. The discolored skin feels odd. It's not really sore, but very sensitive when I type on the keyboard.

Chaz is still standing there, fidgeting with something behind my computer.

I dial Stacy's work before a customer can call. Her friend Lisa tells me that she never came into work today. She had called in sick. She wondered why I didn't know.

It's the hardest day of work since the time I drank a fifth of Jack Daniels the night before and came in with only three hours of sleep.

Stacy isn't there when I get home. There are grocery bags on the kitchen counter. A note saying she'll be back later. I take another shower. Try to wash the dirt out of my fingernails, without much luck. My reddened fingertips are extra sensitive under the hot water. Yeah, they're bruised up pretty bad. They'll probably hurt even worse tomorrow, and that shitty call center job requires fast typing while the customers are on the line. Screw them.

I eat a Hot Pocket and wait around for Stacy to come home, but get tired of sitting on the couch watching awful standup comedians on Comedy Central who talk more about their lame political views than tell jokes. I walk to the bedroom, my feet sticky against the skeleton residue, and go to sleep.

I hear Stacy come home at about three in the morning. I get out of bed, wondering where the heck she's been. She has a bunch of shopping bags that fill the living room floor.

"You're going back in," she says.

I don't think so.

"What's all this stuff?" I ask.

"Supplies," she says.

"Where the heck were you all day?"

"Getting this," she tells me, digging in a bag to retrieve a cigarette carton. She opens it, pulls out a wad of newspaper, and gives it to me like a birthday present.

I unravel it. It's a gun.

"You'll be able to fight them," she says.

"Fight who?" I ask.

"The skeletons," she says. "If they give you trouble."

"I'm not going back in there," I say.

"Are you kidding?" she says. "This is the most fascinating thing that's ever happened to me. Maybe the most fascinating thing that's ever happened to anyone. You're going to be my explorer. You're going to chart the world for me."

"What?"

"And I'm going to write the book about it," she says. "Steve, I've finally realized what I want to do with my life. I knew there was a reason why I was special. This is what I've been preparing myself for all these years."

"I'm not as adventurous as you are," I say.

"Don't worry," she says. "You just have to go a little

farther than last time. And then tomorrow you can go a little farther than that. And then a little farther, and so on. Eventually, we can assemble a team to accompany you."

"Are you going crazy?" I ask her. "A team? What, are you going to invite some spelunkers over and spread your legs for them?"

"You're not taking this seriously," she says.

"I'm taking this very seriously," I say. "I just don't think you hear what you're saying."

"It's the chance of a lifetime," she says. "It'll be danger-ous, but it's worth the risk."

I sit on the couch and put a throw pillow on my lap.

"Look," she says. "I got you a digital camera, so you can take pictures. And walkie-talkies, so we can stay in communication. And climbing gear. I'd like to get a video camera later on. Perhaps there's even a way I can watch the feed on a monitor from out here."

"How is that stuff even going to fit inside of you?" I say. "I barely fit in myself, and I had to be shaved and greased down."

"You'll still go in naked," she says. "But I got this vinyl bag that we can tie to your ankle. It'll slide through easily if we oil it. I bought tons of lubricant, too."

She empties a bag full of bottles of baby oils and tubs of petroleum jelly.

"I also got you a sleeping bag and some food," she says, "if you want to camp out over night."

"I'm not camping out in your vagina overnight," I tell her.

"Not in my vagina," she says. "In my womb."

CHAPTER TEN

It isn't hard for her to persuade me. She knows I'll do anything for her. The next thing I know, I'm back in her vagina, crawling through the flesh tunnel with a bag tied to my ankle.

"Can you hear me?" Stacy asks through the walkie-talkie.

I can hear her all around me.

"Yeah," I tell her.

I can feel her smile. She's so excited.

When I peek my head out of the other end, I brace myself carefully. I don't want to get shot out again. I told Stacy not to masturbate while I'm in here. Last time it could have killed me. She agreed, but seemed pretty disappointed. I'm surprised she didn't do it anyway, just to tease me.

The world looks about the same. The sky is still cloudy and purplish. My axe is still in the side of the cliff. The ladder is still in pieces on the ground.

I hammer a spike into the side of the cliff. It bleeds a little. Then I attach a chord to the peg and propel down.

"I'm in," I tell Stacy.

"Are you safe?" she asks, her voice is accompanied by static.

"Yeah," I tell her.

I open the greasy bag and pull out a towel to wipe off all the petroleum jelly. I insisted on taking that along. Then I put on some clothes and hiking boots. And a thick jacket. Stacy was nice enough to get me a new jacket to keep warm. I put the pistol in the jacket pocket. I've also got a hunting knife that I strap to my ankle.

What else have I got here . . .

Not much. The digital camera. A few energy bars. A water bottle. Stacy agreed I didn't have to stay overnight, so I left the sleeping bag behind. But she wants me to stay as long as I can. I'll see what I can do.

I put everything in my jacket pockets and leave the bag by the side of the cliff. I take a picture of the fleshy entrance, take a picture of the landscape. Then I urinate against a tree.

"What are you doing?" Stacy asks.

"Nothing," I say. "Just about to move on."

I decide to follow the old fence and the cliff rather than enter the forest. It's probably easier to get lost in the forest.

"Keep talking . . . me," Stacy says, static cutting into her words.

"You're going to distract me," I say. "I need to stay alert."

"I'm anxious," she says.

I don't respond.

Farther up, the fence ends in a rotten wooden mailbox. I open it up. It is filled with mud. I stand back and take a picture of it. Nearby, there's what appears to be a trail going into the woods. Mostly grown over, but it looks like it could be some kind of path. I take a picture of the trail, too.

"You should have gotten us a pair of those camera

phones," I tell Stacy.

"I know, I . . . ." she says. ". . . . . tonight."

"I can barely hear you through the static," I say. "You should have gotten better walkie-talkies."

I hear her trying to talk but there's too much static to make out the words. I try walking back along the cliff until it clears up. It doesn't clear up.

"Stacy," I say.

She says something. I think she's trying to tell me to keep going.

I turn off the walkie, put it in my jacket, and take the trail into the forest. Branches have grown over parts of it and I find myself hunched over, walking through, scraping my arms and neck on thorny twigs.

I wonder what kind of trees they are. They look normal enough, but maybe they're different than the trees on the outside world. Maybe there's some small difference that makes them unusual. I take a picture of a tree.

The trail widens a little once I get through the trees. Still grown in a bit with grass. Farther down, it meets with another trail. A crossroads. The other trail is also overgrown like it hasn't been used in ages, but it's much wider. The path I'm on seems to disappear into the trees up ahead, so I take the new route. It brings me into a clearing.

The whole place is silent and motionless. No wind. No thunder in the clouds. No birds chirping. I check the gun in my pocket, make sure I know how to work the safety. I'm not experienced with guns. I don't even know what kind this one is. It looks almost fake. Like some kind of movie prop. Not sure how many bullets it has. There's a clip in there. Nine bullets maybe? Twelve? I have no idea.

My best defense if I come across anything dangerous will be to run away.

I put the gun back in my pocket and take another picture of the surroundings. The pictures look pretty good so far when I scan through them. Just like ordinary photos taken in the real world.

After the clearing, I get to a dirt road. It doesn't look very well-traveled either, but it is a road. There is also a river here, but I don't hear the sound of water. I go to it and take a picture. The water is green and reddish. Filled with algae. The water doesn't seem to be moving. It stretches into the distance, but it's as still as a pond.

I take a picture of it, then check the walkie-talkie. It's still all static.

"Stacy?"

No response at all.

My fingers are all itchy. The red fingertips feel like the circulation is cut off and oxygen isn't getting to them. Pins and needles. I shake them and clench fists, then try to ignore them.

I take the dirt road. It curves through the forest. Then widens up. I eat an energy bar. There are clacking noises up ahead, echoing through the woods. I pull out the gun and continue. The noises get louder as I go. It sounds like breaking tree branches.

Something is moving up ahead. A figure walking across my path, strolling through the woods. That girl I saw outside the cabin. She's smacking trees with a stick as she walks.

I take the safety off.

This time, I don't hide. Just stand here. She's not fifty feet from me, but she doesn't notice me. Just walking through the woods. Once she's out of sight I jog up the trail to where she was standing. I see her strolling between the trees, smacking branches with . . . it's not a stick. It's a skeletal arm. She swings it around, stumbling through the forest in some kind of daze, her paper-white butt jiggling as she walks.

CHAPTER ELEVEN

I follow the girl through the woods, keeping my distance. Her walk is very odd. It's like her footsteps don't have any weight. Stacy's right. She's like a ghost.

There are still clacking sounds in the woods, echoing around me. It isn't just the girl hitting the trees as she walks. Must be the trees themselves. Or maybe it's something Stacy is doing from outside.

I lose her. She disappears in the trees ahead. I push forward, putting my hands in my jacket pockets to hide the gun. Up ahead, the clacking noises grow louder. I get to another dirt road. To the right, there is a bridge and farther down there appear to be buildings. I don't see the girl on the road in either direction.

I pull out the camera and take some pictures.

The bridge is wrought iron, with thick black wires twisted into spirals on the sides. It was once artistically designed, but now it seems melted, burned. It squeals at me when I step on it.

The clacking noises are furious around me. I look over the side of the bridge, into the crevasse . . .

Skeletons.

There are dozens of them down there, animated like the one that came out of Stacy in the bedroom. They race through the gravel toward me, staring up at me with hollow eyes, trying to climb up the sides of the crevasse to get to me.

I keep the gun in my pocket. There's too many of them. If they can get out of there I'd have to run. I wait to see what they do, but they just scrape at the sides of the rock wall, unable to climb it. Many skeletons don't bother trying, just wandering through the reddish moss. There are many bones down there, and pieces of bones, scattered across the landscape.

I take a picture of them, like they are animals on display at a zoo.

One skeleton just stands there, watching me as I cross the squealing bridge to the buildings on the other side.

It's a small town up ahead. A village. Just as quiet and dead as the log cabin in the woods. But these buildings are different. They seem to have been made by the same architect who built the bridge. Most of the houses are wrought iron. They look melted, twisted, burned. The windows are curled and wavy. One of them bubbles outwards. Even the doors and doorways are warped. Some are wide on the top of the frame, then thin at the bottom where they meet the floor. Other doors are so distorted that you couldn't possibly open them.

One building is without a door. I step inside. The insides are also black, crispy, everything made of wrought iron. The floor, the furniture. There are chairs warped and twisted into curly designs. A table that looks like an egg with a broken yolk.

There are shelves here filled with dolls, just like the log cabin. The dolls are also black and warped, like they've been burned and turned to charcoal. I grab one. It is hard like metal. I don't think it is wrought iron, though.

It is something else.

In the next room, there are melty black statues of people. A mother holding a child, the baby dripping through her arms like wet dough. A man in a rocking chair, his head ballooned and folding over.

I take a picture of them.

I go through other buildings. There aren't any people. Just distorted wrought iron statues of people. Dancers with limbs stretched out like they were made of taffy, an old man with boiled skin like a leper, a little girl that has mostly become a puddle on the ground.

I take pictures of all of them.

The town continues on, up a winding hill. Ahead, there are also sculptures of wrought iron trees, wrought iron benches, wrought iron fences. I take a picture of the road ahead, but don't follow it. I think this has been more than enough for one day. I don't think I'm ready to explore anymore of this world alone.

Stacy's going to have to find a team of explorers to accompany me if she wants me to return.

CHAPTER TWELVE

Before I get back to the bridge, a soft breeze creeps down the road, carrying with it a woman's cries.

I look back. The crying is coming from somewhere in the town.

Could it be that ghost girl?

I follow the cries, listening. Stacy thinks that the ghost girl was her imaginary friend when she was a kid, all grown up. But do ghosts grow up? Maybe there are many ghosts here that look the way she does. Maybe Stacy's ghost friend is also here, somewhere, still a little girl.

Up ahead, the cries turn to wails. I walk up the hill, deeper into the town. The houses are much larger up here. They are small, but are two or three stories high, their roofs stretch over the road above me like trees. I take more pictures.

The cries are coming from one of these houses. I can hear them coming out of a window. When I slam open the square metal door, the cries stop. I search the ground floor. It is empty of statues and furniture. There's nobody here. I take the winding stairs. They are so melted and curly that I can hardly climb them, and so thin in places that I can only fit one foot on each step.

I hear crying again at the top of the stairs. Not loudly, though. Just gentle sobbing, coming from a bedroom at the end of a rolling hall.

Peeking my head inside, there is a black statue of a child curled up in the corner, as if crying into its knees. I enter the room. In another corner, facing the statue, is the girl I saw in the woods, also curled on the floor crying into her knees. Still holding the skeletal arm she carries like a walking stick.

I don't speak. Just examine her as she sobs. Her skin is corpse-white with red splotches on her hands, feet, and chest. Short cinnamon hair. And some weird pink horns growing out of her head like long slimy tumors. Just how Stacy described her imaginary friend.

The girl stops crying when she notices me. She blinks a few times. Then sits up.

"You're alive?" she asks.

Her voice is both scratchy and squeaky.

"Yeah," I say.

She kinks her neck and stretches her cheeks into a coy smile.

Then she lunges at me.

I fall back, trying to pull the gun out of my pocket, but she catches me too quickly. She wraps her arms around me and hugs me as tight as she can.

"Alive!" she says.

Just holding me for a while, rocking me back and forth. I don't know what to do but hug her back.

Her skin is like latex. Much more smooth than normal flesh, much squishier as well. She looks at me, flicks her eyelashes. Her eyes are cherry red.

"I love your feel," she says, caressing my cheek with her plastic hands.

She seems so unnatural, but she doesn't look or feel

like a ghost. Her eyes are very large and her mouth is kind of small. She's more like a computer-generated cartoon character.

She steps back from me, her footsteps weightless, her shadow looks all wrong.

No, she's exactly like a CGI character. She's like Jar Jar Binks.

"Why come to me?" asks the girl.

I open my mouth to speak.

"Did you come to play?" asks the girl.

"Sure," I say.

She smiles. Her pointy eyebrows always seem to be curled down, like she's angry or annoyed, even when she smiles.

"What's your name?" she asks.

"Steve," I tell her.

"Ewww," she says. "I hate that!"

I snicker but she doesn't laugh with me, just stares at me with her annoyed eyebrows like I'm the oddest thing she's ever seen.

"What's your name?" I ask.

"Fig," she says.

"Nice name," I tell her.

She looks in another direction for a while like she's forgotten I'm in the room with her.

"Can I take your picture?" I ask.

She's still forgotten about me.

I take her picture. When I check to see how the picture came out on the digital camera, she looks like a still shot from a video game.

"I've been wanting someone to play with," she says.

"Are you all alone?" I ask.

She makes a face at me like something smells funny.

She takes me out into the street.

"There's a rock," she says to me, pointing at a tiny pebble in the road, as though it were something I'd be interested in. "He's dumb."

"Home is better," she says.

We walk farther up the hill. Fig keeps talking to me in her creeky voice about the stupidest things.

"I fell down there," she says, pointing at a patch of dirt.

"That's mean," she says, pointing at a stick in the road.

"Those are funny," she says, pointing at a mushroom patch.

I just walk with her, watching her unnatural footsteps and bouncy latex flesh. She looks like she could be Stacy's age, but seems pretty young. Early twenties. Maybe it's just her personality that makes her seem younger. She doesn't seem to need clothing. Her red feet don't get hurt against the ground. Her skin doesn't shiver when the wind picks up. She doesn't even seem to have nipples or pubic hair to hide. I take another picture of her.

"Do you remember someone named Stacy?" I ask her, interrupting something she was saying about the different names she has for each cloud in the sky.

She says, "Stacy says I don't exist."

"You were friends when you were kids?" I ask.

"Stacy's not my friend," she says, pouting.

We continue up the road. The wrought iron houses become normal houses. I pause to take another picture.

The black metal stops halfway through the homes here. One half is wooden and perfectly constructed. The other half is distorted and black.

I point at the black and ask the girl, "What is that?"

"That's the cancer," she says.

"Cancer?" I ask.

"It took everyone away," she says.

The town ends at the top of the hill, but the path continues.

"Where are we going?" I ask.

"To dinner," she says.

There are skeletons walking in the forest, clacking their bones against trees as they move.

"Friendly zephrans," she says to me.

The skeletons don't pay attention to us, dancing in the woods like they're held up by strings.

Fig lives in the mansion at the top of the hill. A blue-violet doll house as big as a ski lodge.

"Everyone else lives there," she says.

CHAPTER THIRTEEN

Fig doesn't live alone in this world as I suspected. There are other people here, living in the mansion.

"All old," she says. "I can't play with any of them."

They are all just as alien as Fig, some of them more so. They are also like three-dimensional cartoon characters. And just like cartoon characters, they are proportioned oddly. Some have large gorilla bodies with tiny little legs. Some are thin with long noodle arms.

She gathers them all to dinner so they can meet me. I sit at the end of the table next to Fig. There are a little over a dozen of them. Many of them couples, and the couples all look similar. The green spiky man and woman look to be married. The yellow long noses look to be a couple, and an even older yellow long-nosed couple sits across from them. Probably their parents. Only one of them looks like Fig. An old woman, sitting next to her, with deep jowls. Probably her mother or grandmother. Everyone is very sluggish and droopy. All of them very old.

I take pictures of them, then introduce myself.

They just look at me for a second when I speak, then look away.

"They don't understand you," Fig says. "Only I talk like you."

The people speak under their breaths, mumbling, I can't even hear them. Fig speaks to them in their language. It sounds kind of like Chinese.

"I told them you're my new playmate," she says.

They all nod at me, talking in loud crackling voices

amongst themselves.

After maybe twenty minutes of socializing, we are served by Fig's relative. Only we aren't served food, we are served crafts. Some of the people get balls of yarn, some people get puzzles, most of the people get dolls to paint. I get modeling clay.

Fig sticks her tongue out at my clay, like it's gross.

She's bouncing in her seat excited to work on painting a skull that chatters its teeth at her.

"I thought we were going to have food?" I ask her.

She doesn't know what I'm talking about.

We sit here for what seems like three hours before Fig's mom collects our crafts and takes them away. I tried to make a sculpture of a cowboy boot but it wasn't turning out so I just made an abstract spiky snake. Fig's relative looks at it like it's something pornographic.

All of the people get up out of their chairs and stretch, stepping away from the table. I slip away when they aren't looking, go out on the porch.

I take pictures of the surroundings. From up here, I can see almost everything. I can see the cliff where I entered this world. It stretches all the way around us. Like we're in a crater. The entire world is only about twenty square miles.

I need to get back. Stacy's probably wondering why I'm taking so long.

I try to get a hold of her on the walkie-talkie.

"Stacy, are you there?" I say.

But it's still static.

"What are you doing?" I hear Fig's creeky voice behind me.

I turn around, putting the walkie back in my pocket.

"I'm leaving," I tell her.

"You're not leaving," she says.

"I need to get back to Stacy," I say.

"But we haven't even played yet," she says.

"I thought we just did," I say.

She wiggles her nose at me. "We just had dinner. I said I wanted to play after dinner."

"Dinner took too long," I tell her. "I need to go now."

"But mom said you could play with me forever if I want," she says.

"Maybe another time," I say.

I turn and walk away from her.

"NO!" she shrieks at me.

I keep moving.

Once I get down to the black metal houses, I look back. She's following me, angry-faced, fists-clenched. What a freak. I'm definitely not coming back into this world by myself again.

"Zephrans! Zephrans! Zephrans!" she cries out behind me.

I turn around. She's facing the woods, looking at the skeletons that we passed earlier. They are coming out of the forest toward her. She turns and looks at me, burning red eyes at me. The skeletons come up behind her and stop moving. They seem to be at her command.

"Bring him back," she says.

Then the skeletons charge.

I run.

I could shoot the five skeletons chasing me, but it's easier to just run away. Flying down the hill as fast as I can, I hear clacking noises coming from the buildings I pass. Skeletons are coming out of the forest behind the houses. Up ahead, dozens of skeletal figures stagger down the road toward me. I didn't notice it before, but the skeletons also look computer-generated. Like they just came out of an episode of *Hercules: The Legendary Journeys* starring Kevin Sorbo.

They surround me in the road. I take the safety off my pistol and charge into them, firing point blank at their skulls when they get too close. Bones explode into baking soda as I dart through.

More of them come out of the woods, dozens of them, from all directions. They close in on me. I run out of ammunition and take the hunting knife from my ankle. I stab at one of the skeletons and the knife gets stuck inside of its nose hole.

As I'm trying to pull it out, skeletons grab my arms, wrap around my back, seize my legs. The knife falls out of my hand and I'm picked up off the ground. Clacking noises all around me as they raise me over their heads.

Their rubbery bones cut off the circulation in my elbows as they bring me back to Fig.

"Take him to the mine," she says. "Nobody will hear him there."

She leads the skeletal crew into the forest, carrying me for what seems like a mile. I struggle to free myself, but there's too many of them. I'm taken down into a field of orange flowers, stripped naked. Then they throw me down a mine shaft.

CHAPTER FOURTEEN

I'm not too hurt when I fall. The ground is blubbery and I bounce off like a trampoline. I'm about thirty feet down. There's no way to get back up. It's more like a well than a mineshaft.

Fig looks down at me from the circle of sky.

"You're not going anywhere," she says, her voice more scratchy than squeaky now.

"I need to go home," I tell her. "I don't belong here."

"You have to play with me forever," she says.

"I need to get back to Stacy," I tell her.

"She'll forget about you," she says. "Like she forgot about me."

"But I love her!"

She stares down at me for awhile. Then she leaves.

I wait for hours. She doesn't come back. I'm trapped. Just standing here, under the light from above.

There's not a night time or day time in this world. It's always in-between. Like dawn or dusk, without a sun in the sky.

I sit down. The ground is wet and fleshy. I rub my hand on it. It is warm.

It's Stacy's flesh. I must be at the bottom of their world, where the earth meets her body. What the hell am I going to do? What if I never get out of here? What if I never see Stacy again?

I lie on my belly and embrace the fleshy ground, to get closer to my love. My cheeks become wet with tears, or maybe it's just sweat rising out of the skin below me. I drift into sleep, absorbing the sound of Stacy's heartbeat vibrating through my entire body.

Time passes. It seems like weeks.

My skin is changing. It's becoming rubbery. The redness of my fingertips has spread down to my wrists. My chest and feet are also red. Slimy balls are growing out of the sides of my head. I'm becoming like Fig.

I haven't eaten anything since my last energy bar but I haven't been hungry or thirsty at all. I should have died of thirst by now. I believe my new skin is absorbing nutrients from the atmosphere. Stacy's body must feed this world in the way it would feed a baby in its womb. People don't need to eat or drink here.

I've taken to talking to the ground as if it is Stacy. I tell her how happy I am to still be with her, even though we can't see each other. I'm sure she feels the same way, comforting her lonely nights by knowing that I am still inside her, thinking about her.

After my voice starts to get scratchy, I just speak to her in my head.

71

I awake to a cracking sound coming from the back of my head. Then a tearing sound down my spine as if my flesh is being unzipped from my neck to my pelvis. I'm unable to move as my body opens up. My bones and muscles separate. A skeleton crawls out of me.

I leap away, kicking at the creature scurrying across the sweaty ground. My body is lighter. I feel my back. The wound is already healing. But my insides . . . hollow. My bones have become animated and detached themselves from my body.

The skeleton squats down in front of me, examining my face, touching its own face with bloody fingers. It looks as confused as I am, wondering what it is doing outside of me. It doesn't have a brain or any vital organs. I'm not sure how it's able to function or think. I'm not sure how I'm able to function or move without any bones . . .

But I am able to move. My body feels almost weightless. My fingers curl around my wrist like rubber snakes. My head is softer without a skull, but it still feels as if something is in there guarding my brain. A thin layer of cartilage maybe. It feels firm but flexible, like a dolphin's back.

The skeleton claws at my wormy toes like a kitten.

"No," I tell the skeleton.

It clacks its teeth at me.

"Bad skeleton," I say.

The skeleton wags its pelvic bone like a tail.

CHAPTER FIFTEEN

After a couple days of playing catch with the skeleton, training it not to bite my feet, trying not to move so much so that the enormous wound on my back will fully heal, Fig finally returns.

I'm completely like her now. The long gooey horns, the white and red-splotched flesh, the large eyes and small mouth, the bouncy latex skin. My movements are just as unnatural as hers, like I'm claymated or computer-generated.

"You're like me now," Fig says from above. Her screaky voice is like needles to my ears. "You *do* belong here."

She drops a rope down to me.

"You have to play with me," she says. "No running away?"

"I'll be good," I say. My voice is alien. It is just as squeaky as hers. My voice box must have been turned to rubber.

The rope is easy to climb with my new lightweight body. I could probably even climb the cliff with ease. I look back to see the skeleton climbing the rope after me, chattering its teeth at my ankles.

As soon as I get out, I'm going to take off. I need to get back to Stacy. Hopefully, she'll still recognize me when I come out. Hopefully, I'll be able to change back.

Halfway up, Fig says, "Don't think you can run away. Good zephrans are guarding the bridge. Bad zephrans are under the bridge."

I keep climbing.

The skeletons aren't going to stop me. If I have to start cutting off Fig's fingers until she orders them to go away, I will. Even if I have to kill her. Nothing's going to stop me from getting back to my love.

Outside the mineshaft, Fig feels my new skin. I check it out myself, in the new lighting. My nipples and body hair have disappeared. The hair on my head has grown in. I wonder if my eyes and hair have become red. Stacy's going to freak out when she sees me.

"Let's go play!" Fig says, like an excited little girl.

She's such a sad lonely creature. No wonder she's always been crying, weeping out of Stacy's vagina for the past twenty-odd years.

I follow her through the field of orange flowers, just waiting for the right time to grab her. There aren't any skeletons with her, but that doesn't mean they aren't around. My skeleton follows behind us. I'm not sure whether its on my side or hers.

"This is going to be fun!" she creaky-says.

"What game do you want to play?" I creaky-say.

She hops up and down at me. I go to grab her, but I fall over as the ground starts rumbling. An earthquake.

"What's going on?" I ask.

"Is this the one?" she says, looking around.

I watch the trees thrashing over us.

"Follow me," she says. "Just in case."

We run up the hill, stumbling on the shaky ground, trying to get to the highest peak in the valley. We enter the mansion and go up to the roof, where all the other cartoonish people are standing.

They are all looking in one direction, in the distance.

"Is this the one? Is this the one?" Fig yells over the rumbling.

What the hell is going on?

I stand up on a table, to see over the crowd, to see what they are looking at. They are all looking toward the cliff where I came from, but there's nothing of interest over there . . .

Wait a minute . . . Stacy's not . . .

A geyser erupts out of the side of the cliff, a burst of white fluid. Then another burst of white fluid. Then another.

She is!

Stacy's . . . having sex!

I can't keep my mouth closed. Like an avalanche, the valley fills with some guy's cum. Some guy Stacy's cheating on me with. It's only been a few weeks! And I'm still inside her! What is she doing!

I step down from the table as the earthquake calms down. She didn't even use a condom. What the hell is she thinking? What if she gets a disease? She wouldn't have sex with me without a condom for months after we had been dating, after she sent me to the doctor to make sure I was completely STD free. How could she . . .

The crowd keeps staring off into the distance.

"This could be it," Fig says, pointing at a crater a couple miles away from the cliff.

The lake of sperm oozes across the landscape, flooding the trees, some houses. As the white gook enters the crater, the people hold their breath and look up at the sky.

"Watch for it," Fig tells me, pointing at the clouds.

I look up.

The clouds scatter, as if wiped away with a rag, revealing the dome-shaped purple sky. Then the entire crowd leaps up with insane cheering as a pink film stretches across the atmosphere, covering us like a blanket.

"It happened! It happened!" Fig cries.

I don't have to ask to know what they are cheering about.

I already know . . .

Stacy's been impregnated.

I drop to my butt and look away. My skeleton is in a corner, smacking spiders out of webs and chattering its teeth at them.

I place my rubbery hands in my face. The tears feel foreign against my skin.

"Ha!" Fig squints her face, pointing at me. "You can't leave now!"

I wipe my eyes.

"I told you," she says. "You're going to play with me forever! Mom said so! She's never wrong!"

She's right. I can't leave. Not for a decade or two, at least.

The impregnation cut off the tunnel between this world and the other. We're no longer inside Stacy's body, we're inside of her baby's. The opening on the cliff's face has disappeared. I'm trapped in here until a new one opens. Once Stacy's child is old enough to let me through. And even then, I don't know if my new body will be able to survive out there.

I wander through the mansion, pacing the musty halls, ignoring the inhabitants, pushing Fig and my skeleton away from me when they try to follow.

How could Stacy do this to me? Not even a single month has gone by and she's already sleeping with somebody else . . . She's the one who forced me to come here. Why didn't she send somebody in to look for me?

This can't be right. She loves me. She would never do this to me.

Maybe it wasn't her fault. Maybe she was raped. Or maybe it was some kind of accident. Maybe some guy had volunteered to come into this world to search for me but accidentally ejaculated while trying to climb through her vaginal tunnel . . . Or maybe the guy never believed her about the world in her womb. Maybe he just thought Stacy was some crazy chick and thought he could take advantage of her. "You want me to enter your vagina? Sure, no problem!" Or when he was trying to climb inside, maybe Stacy just got swept up in the moment. She could have been so turned on as he tried entering her that they ended up screwing instead of saving me.

That's something I always hated about Stacy. She's the type of person who always gets swept up in the moment. Whenever she's having a good time with her friends, she'll always forget about the plans she had with me. Whenever guys flirt with her, she always flirts back, even when I'm standing right next to her. I know she loves me, but sometimes her emotions blind her and carry her away.

For all I know, she could have done it to tease me. It's just like Stacy to get turned on by the idea of having sex with some strange guy while I'm trapped inside of her. I'm sure that idea would have turned her on. I always hated her sick fetishes. Like how she sometimes liked to choke me or choke herself while fucking. She had some kind of neck fetish. I especially hated when she would lie on top of me and fuck my throat. She liked the feeling of my Adam's apple against her clit, and liked to choke me with her thighs. She also made me hum while she was grinding my neck so that my voice box would work like a vibrator.

I want to leave her for sleeping with another guy. I want to kick her out of my house and tell her I never want to see her again. But I can't. I'll never be able to leave her for as long as I live.

CHAPTER SIXTEEN

I leave the mansion and stroll down the hill, trying not to look into the clear pink sky. It reminds me too much of Stacy.

After passing a few houses, I realize I'm being followed by Fig. I stop and sneer back at her as she approaches, clenching my fists as if to punch her in the face if she gets too close.

"What?" I yell.

"It's bright out here," she says, completely unfazed by my anger.

She wiggles her nostrils at the air, as if trying to smell the pink of the sky.

"Let's get out of the bright," she says, wandering into an abandoned lime green house on the left.

I watch her disappear into the house without looking back. I wait in the street for a while, staring at my rubbery red feet. She doesn't come back out to see what's keeping me. She's so odd. I decide to leave and continue down the road, but something prevents me from going. Something drives me to go into the house with Fig. Maybe I just don't want to go to the bottom of the hill. There are skeletons down there, and the neighborhood of black deformities, not to mention there's an enormous lake of some guy's rancid cum. Maybe I have nothing better to do. Maybe I just don't want to be alone.

I find her upstairs, squatting in the hallway. Her shiny rump sticking in the air as she pulls on carpet fragments.

"They like the attention," she says.

I realize I am checking out her ass when I see my reflection in one of her white butt cheeks, and quickly turn away before she catches me. I pass her and enter one of the bedrooms. It is filled with three beds, three dressers, and a large window with chainmail curtains. A kid's room.

"We should play now," Fig says behind me.

I shrug.

Fig attempts to kiss me. I turn my head away and she begins sucking on my neck with latex lips.

I push her away. "What are you doing?"

She pulls me by the hand toward one of the kiddie beds.

"We're playing," she says.

Her wormy fingers curl around my penis. Playing? This is what she meant by playing? She slips her tongue into my tiny mouth as she fondles my squishy member into erection.

I shove her away. "No."

She looks confused at me. "But we're supposed to play!"

"I don't want to play with you."

"You're not for her anymore," she says, rubbing my arms. "You're for me."

She knows I'm thinking about Stacy. I clench my fists, my face turning red in Fig's cartoon eyes. I want to hurt someone. I want someone to feel my pain, physically. I want to make somebody pay for all that's happened to me.

As my rage builds, Fig watches me, masturbating at me. A vein in my forehead twitches as she wipes her greasy fingers across my lips and nostrils, just like Stacy used to do. Stacy always liked to see my reaction to the taste of her, to the smell of her, even though she knew it pissed me off.

But Fig tastes different than Stacy. She is the flavor of roses. Flower sweat. Her scent fills my lungs and gives my breath a fluffy texture.

Something in my brain snaps and I find myself lunging at Fig. I grab her by the elbows and squeeze her as hard as I can, trying to crush pain into her snake-like arms. Then I throw her to the ground as hard as I can, pin her down, and choke her the way Stacy used to choke me.

I stop when I see her face. She's looking at me, confused. Not hurt or scared, just not sure what I'm trying to do. I take my hands away from her throat and look away from her, shamefaced.

"That's not how you do it," she creaky-says beneath me.

I feel her grabbing at my erection and pointing it into her crotch. She rubs it against her slippery opening, her breath cold on my neck. Then she grabs my butt with both hands and pulls me into her.

Inside, it's like hot jelly or maybe rubber cement. She writhes under me with a crooked smile, gripping my hips and pulsing against me. We kiss each other with our tiny mouths, pressing against each other's smooth plastic skin. My rubbery penis pumps into her latex vagina, creating a loud squeaky sound that echoes through the musty room. She doesn't have any nipples, but I still lick her breasts as if they were there. It doesn't seem to do anything for her, though.

Our sex feels far from human. More like snail sex. Or jellyfish sex. Or Japanese anime sex. Our boneless bodies twisting into inhuman positions. It's incredibly strange, but it might just be the best sex I've ever had.

The orgasm ripples through my entire body, like ocean waves under my skin. My testicles crack open and release two raw eggs that goo up and out of my shaft into Fig. She closes her eyes and leans back as the yolks sink deep inside of her.

As the yolks pop, she lets out a sigh and curls her head deep into my shoulder, tears dripping down her cheek, pooling on my neck.

I wake up after a short snooze. Fig's cinnamon hair in my face, her drool on my chest. We're hardly able to both fit on the kid's bed, but we're so twisted around each other that neither of us are in danger of falling off. I un-pretzel myself and slip out of the room, through the chainmail curtains onto the balcony. The warmth of the bright pink sky glazes my face.

This place isn't a ghost world, just a beaten down lonely world. It must have been around for centuries, getting passed from host to host, mother to daughter, generation after generation. I can't even begin to imagine how this place was even created. Perhaps it was created by some kind of cosmic accident. Perhaps it was bio-engineered by some kind of Asian Frankenstein. Or perhaps it's some sort of evolutionary mutation. Perhaps, a long time ago, in Asia, where Stacy was born, there was a village that had too many people but not enough food. Perhaps this situation went on for so long that evolution had to step in and do something about it. Perhaps a few mutant females were born, each containing fertile worlds inside of them. Worlds that many of the villagers could move into. Worlds where its occupants wouldn't need food or water. Worlds that could sustain several villages. All that would be needed is to feed and protect the female hosts of the worlds.

I look out to the blackened houses down the road. Fig called it "the cancer." Perhaps Stacy's mother had a disease that spread through her body, destroying her insides as well as the world within her. Perhaps she passed the world onto Stacy and gave birth to her before the cancer could destroy the entire world. Perhaps her mother died of the disease before she had the chance to tell Stacy about the secret place hidden in her belly. When she was adopted by her American parents and brought to California, Stacy was forever cut off from the truth. That is, if anyone still knows the truth.

I'm pretty sure that the world was created so long ago that nobody really knows the truth anymore. Even the inhabitants of this world. After so many generations, the truth has probably been twisted, turned into myth. These people have been detached from the outside world for so long that they probably doubt it even exists. They probably know as much about it as we know of Heaven.

"I'm going to miss them," Fig says, stepping onto the balcony behind me.

She's looking at the sky. I think she's talking about the clouds. She had names for all of them. She talks about them as if they were real people.

"They were my friends," she says, a tear on her cheek.

I wrap my arms around her. I don't know why. It's ridiculous that she's crying over the loss of some clouds, but in a way I guess it's kind of cute.

"You're here, though," she says. "You're better."

I wipe her cheek with my thumb. It makes a sound like a windshield wiper.

"You love me back," she says.

I freeze at the word *love* and step away from her. "I never said I love you. We hardly know each other."

"But you changed for me," she says, petting my slimy horns, touching my skin. "You're mine."

"I didn't want to change," I say. "It just happened."

"It happened because you belong to me."

CHAPTER SEVENTEEN

Fig and I get married, eventually.

I'm in love with her now. Maybe even more than I ever loved Stacy. Her crackling voice drives me wild. Her big cartoon eyes entrap me for hours.

"It was written," Fig's mom says, in her language, watching us as we move into the south wing of the mansion together. A long abandoned section that we are fixing into our home.

My mother-in-law's language is Thai, or some kind of language that has evolved from Thai. I've been trying to learn it, but it'll take time before I can speak fluently. Fig tries to teach it to me but her attention rarely stays focused on one project long enough to accomplish anything. I'm not sure where she learned English. At first, I thought she picked it up from Stacy when they were kids, but I have found some books written in English on some of the shelves in the mansion. Somebody who migrated to this world must have known the English language at some point. Maybe Fig's father or an uncle.

It's difficult to get straight answers out of Fig sometimes. She's definitely an odd one, but I love her so much. I love everything about her.

This is the way Fig wakes me up in the morning:

First, she goes outside for a walk. Once she comes back, she has a basket filled with something to give me. Usually a type of flower or a bundle of rocks or snails. She'll put them on the blanket in some kind of design. It's always the same design, but I don't know what it means.

It's some Thai symbol, but I believe it means love. After that she rubs the red tip of her nose against the red tip of my nose until I wake up and give her a kiss.

If anybody would have done these things to me in the outside world, even Stacy, I would have been annoyed. But with Fig, they make me happy. She's so cute.

But I think the reason I'm in love with her, the reason I think she's so cute, is because of what she's done to me.

The people of this world are all born with unique DNA. They are born a species of one. Sometimes they match their parents, like Fig, but usually they are born completely alien from all others. When a female is within the vicinity of a male she releases super-charged pheromones that alter the man's DNA to match her own. He will mutate into the male counterpart of her species. Then they become a species of two.

I believe the pheromones also release chemicals into the male's brain that act as aphrodisiacs. Because every time Fig and I are together now I can't help but jump all over her. It's more than the usual horniness I would get in the outside world. It is some kind of deep uncontrollable urge to mate with the only female of my species. Sometimes these feelings make it frustrating to be around Fig. Other times, they make me happy, euphoric. They make me love life, love myself, and they especially make me love Fig more than anything.

Fig is pregnant, her belly stretched out like a water balloon. She smiles, squinting the bridge of her nose at me, as I put new logs on the fire to keep her warm.

My skeleton is curled up on a rug next to her rocking chair. Fig pets the back of its skull. Its chattering teeth like a kitten's purr.

I dig through old crates, looking for interesting scraps for dinner tomorrow. In one of the crates in the back, I find the sculpture I made the day I met Fig and her family. I also find Stacy's digital camera, and the walkie-talkie.

The walkie still has batteries. I wonder if Stacy still has the other one. For weeks after she became impregnated, I tried contacting her on this. But there was always static. The tunnel to this world has been shut off, so I couldn't get anything through to her at all.

Just out of curiosity, I take the walkie to the roof, sneak away from Fig while she's basking in the warmth of the fire with her eyes closed. The snores of the old mutant people fill the house. I'm careful not to wake them.

Outside, the sky is clear of clouds. I can see the outline of the baby's arm up there, waving down at me from the heavens.

"Stacy?" I speak into the walkie.

The baby's arm jerks in the sky.

I repeat *Stacy, are you there?* a few times. Just enjoying the landscape, breathing in the fresh air, not expecting anybody to answer.

But somebody does answer. It is distant at first. Hard to make out. But it gets clearer.

"Steve . . ." the voice says.

It's Stacy. Her voice almost seems alien to me now. As my voice must sound alien to her.

"I'm still here," I tell her.

There is a pause.

"Steve, is that really you? You sound so strange . . ."

I can hear her crying.

"I miss you so much," she says.

"I miss you, too," I tell her.

"I think about you every night," she says. "I've kept batteries in the walkie-talkie just in case you ever wanted to reach me. I never gave up hope for you."

Yeah, that's why she fucked some guy only a few weeks after I went missing . . .

"How's the father of your child?" I ask her.

She pauses.

"I don't know," she says. "It was just some guy I met at a bar. I was so upset. I didn't know what I was doing."

I sit down in a wicker chair.

"How's your lover?" she asks, almost annoyed.

"Fig?" I ask. "She's doing fine. We're pregnant. She should be due any day now. Same as you, I believe."

"She was my imaginary friend, wasn't she?" she asks. "From when I was a kid?"

"Yeah," I say.

"She was so lonely," she says. "Her cries always calling out to me, begging me to send her somebody to love. She was always so sad and angry. But then, after you went inside me, there wasn't crying anymore. There was singing. She was happy. She was in love."

My lips squeak as they rub against the receiver.

"I knew it," she says. "I knew, when you didn't come

back, you two had fallen in love and you decided to stay with her. Hearing her happy voice day after day made me so jealous. Then it pissed me off. I hated you for what you did to me. I fucked the first guy I could find, hoping I would drown you two in his cum. I thought I did, too. Her voice stopped coming out of me. My vagina was silent. I felt horrible. I thought I killed you. I would have sent somebody in to see if you were okay, but it doesn't stretch anymore. I was hoping you were still alive in there. Inside of me."

"Yeah," I tell her. "But the world isn't inside of you anymore. It is inside of your baby."

"I want to see you again, Steve," she says. "I don't care how long it takes. Maybe you can come out of my daughter when she grows up. You can be with me again."

"I'm not exactly human anymore, Stacy," I say. "I don't think I can return to that world."

"Then I'll come to you . . ."

"Stacy," I say. "I loved you more than the whole world, but I've got a responsibility here. I've got people that need me. I've already moved on."

"I know . . ." she says.

"I'm married and have a child coming," I say.

"I know," she says. "But . . ."

She pauses.

"Are you happy?" she asks.

"Yes," I tell her. "I'm very happy."

"I just want you to be happy," she tells me.

"I am," I say.

She cries into the walkie.

"Stacy?" I say.

"Yeah?"

"I'll always be with you . . ."

She continues crying and then the walkie cuts out. I think she turned it off or maybe threw it across the room.

That's another thing I always hated about Stacy. She'd always cut me off in the middle of a conversation for the sake of being dramatic.

THE END

ABOUT THE AUTHOR

Carlton Mellick III is one of the leading authors in the new *Bizarro* genre uprising. Since 2001, his surreal counterculture novels have drawn an international cult following despite the fact that they have been shunned by most libraries and corporate bookstores. He lives in Portland, OR, the bizarro fiction mecca.

Visit him online at **www.carltonmellick.com**

Bizarro books

CATALOG SPRING 2011

Bizarro Books publishes under the following imprints:

www.rawdogscreamingpress.com

www.eraserheadpress.com

www.afterbirthbooks.com

www.swallowdownpress.com

For all your Bizarro needs visit:

WWW.BIZARROCENTRAL.COM

Introduce yourselves to the bizarro fiction genre and all of its authors with the Bizarro Starter Kit series. Each volume features short novels and short stories by ten of the leading bizarro authors, designed to give you a perfect sampling of the genre for only $10.

BB-0X1
"The Bizarro Starter Kit" (Orange)
Featuring D. Harlan Wilson, Carlton Mellick III, Jeremy Robert Johnson, Kevin L Donihe, Gina Ranalli, Andre Duza, Vincent W. Sakowski, Steve Beard, John Edward Lawson, and Bruce Taylor.
236 pages $10

BB-0X2
"The Bizarro Starter Kit" (Blue)
Featuring Ray Fracalossy, Jeremy C. Shipp, Jordan Krall, Mykle Hansen, Andersen Prunty, Eckhard Gerdes, Bradley Sands, Steve Aylett, Christian TeBordo, and Tony Rauch. **244 pages $10**

BB-0X2
"The Bizarro Starter Kit" (Purple)
Featuring Russell Edson, Athena Villaverde, David Agranoff, Matthew Revert, Andrew Goldfarb, Jeff Burk, Garrett Cook, Kris Saknussemm, Cody Goodfellow, and Cameron Pierce **264 pages $10**

BB-001 "The Kafka Effekt" D. Harlan Wilson - A collection of forty-four irreal short stories loosely written in the vein of Franz Kafka, with more than a pinch of William S. Burroughs sprinkled on top. **211 pages $14**

BB-002 "Satan Burger" Carlton Mellick III - The cult novel that put Carlton Mellick III on the map ... Six punks get jobs at a fast food restaurant owned by the devil in a city violently overpopulated by surreal alien cultures. **236 pages $14**

BB-003 "Some Things Are Better Left Unplugged" Vincent Sakwoski - Join The Man and his Nemesis, the obese tabby, for a nightmare roller coaster ride into this postmodern fantasy. **152 pages $10**

BB-004 "Shall We Gather At the Garden?" Kevin L Donihe - Donihe's Debut novel. Midgets take over the world, The Church of Lionel Richie vs. The Church of the Byrds, plant porn and more! **244 pages $14**

BB-005 "Razor Wire Pubic Hair" Carlton Mellick III - A genderless humandildo is purchased by a razor dominatrix and brought into her nightmarish world of bizarre sex and mutilation. **176 pages $11**

BB-006 "Stranger on the Loose" D. Harlan Wilson - The fiction of Wilson's 2nd collection is planted in the soil of normalcy, but what grows out of that soil is a dark, witty, otherworldly jungle... **228 pages $14**

BB-007 "The Baby Jesus Butt Plug" Carlton Mellick III - Using clones of the Baby Jesus for anal sex will be the hip sex fetish of the future. **92 pages $10**

BB-008 "Fishyfleshed" Carlton Mellick III - The world of the past is an illogical flatland lacking in dimension and color, a sick-scape of crispy squid people wandering the desert for no apparent reason. **260 pages $14**

BB-009 **"Dead Bitch Army" Andre Duza** - Step into a world filled with racist teenagers, cannibals, 100 warped Uncle Sams, automobiles with razor-sharp teeth, living graffiti, and a pissed-off zombie bitch out for revenge. **344 pages $16**

BB-010 **"The Menstruating Mall" Carlton Mellick III** - "The Breakfast Club meets Chopping Mall as directed by David Lynch." - Brian Keene **212 pages $12**

BB-011 **"Angel Dust Apocalypse" Jeremy Robert Johnson** - Meth-heads, man-made monsters, and murderous Neo-Nazis. "Seriously amazing short stories..." - Chuck Palahniuk, author of Fight Club **184 pages $11**

BB-012 **"Ocean of Lard" Kevin L Donihe / Carlton Mellick III** - A parody of those old Choose Your Own Adventure kid's books about some very odd pirates sailing on a sea made of animal fat. **176 pages $12**

BB-015 **"Foop!" Chris Genoa** - Strange happenings are going on at Dactyl, Inc, the world's first and only time travel tourism company.
"A surreal pie in the face!" - Christopher Moore **300 pages $14**

BB-020 **"Punk Land" Carlton Mellick III** - In the punk version of Heaven, the anarchist utopia is threatened by corporate fascism and only Goblin, Mortician's sperm, and a blue-mohawked female assassin named Shark Girl can stop them. **284 pages $15**

BB-021 **"Pseudo-City" D. Harlan Wilson** - Pseudo-City exposes what waits in the bathroom stall, under the manhole cover and in the corporate boardroom, all in a way that can only be described as mind-bogglingly irreal. **220 pages $16**

BB-023 **"Sex and Death In Television Town" Carlton Mellick III** - In the old west, a gang of hermaphrodite gunslingers take refuge from a demon plague in Telos: a town where its citizens have televisions instead of heads. **184 pages $12**

BB-027 "Siren Promised" Jeremy Robert Johnson & Alan M Clark
- Nominated for the Bram Stoker Award. A potent mix of bad drugs, bad dreams, brutal bad guys, and surreal/incredible art by Alan M. Clark. **190 pages $13**

BB-030 "Grape City" Kevin L. Donihe - More Donihe-style comedic bizarro about a demon named Charles who is forced to work a minimum wage job on Earth after Hell goes out of business. **108 pages $10**

BB-031 "Sea of the Patchwork Cats" Carlton Mellick III - A quiet dreamlike tale set in the ashes of the human race. For Mellick enthusiasts who also adore The Twilight Zone. **112 pages $10**

BB-032 "Extinction Journals" Jeremy Robert Johnson - An uncanny voyage across a newly nuclear America where one man must confront the problems associated with loneliness, insane dieties, radiation, love, and an ever-evolving cockroach suit with a mind of its own. **104 pages $10**

BB-034 "The Greatest Fucking Moment in Sports" Kevin L. Donihe
- In the tradition of the surreal anti-sitcom Get A Life comes a tale of triumph and agape love from the master of comedic bizarro. **108 pages $10**

BB-035 "The Troublesome Amputee" John Edward Lawson - Disturbing verse from a man who truly believes nothing is sacred and intends to prove it. **104 pages $9**

BB-037 "The Haunted Vagina" Carlton Mellick III - It's difficult to love a woman whose vagina is a gateway to the world of the dead. **132 pages $10**

BB-042 "Teeth and Tongue Landscape" Carlton Mellick III - On a planet made out of meat, a socially-obsessive monophobic man tries to find his place amongst the strange creatures and communities that he comes across. **110 pages $10**

BB-043 **"War Slut" Carlton Mellick III** - Part "1984," part "Waiting for Godot," and part action horror video game adaptation of John Carpenter's "The Thing." **116 pages $10**

BB-045 **"Dr. Identity" D. Harlan Wilson** - Follow the Dystopian Duo on a killing spree of epic proportions through the irreal postcapitalist city of Bliptown where time ticks sideways, artificial Bug-Eyed Monsters punish citizens for consumer-capitalist lethargy, and ultraviolence is as essential as a daily multivitamin. **208 pages $15**

BB-047 **"Sausagey Santa" Carlton Mellick III** - A bizarro Christmas tale featuring Santa as a piratey mutant with a body made of sausages. 124 pages $10

BB-048 **"Misadventures in a Thumbnail Universe" Vincent Sakowski** - Dive deep into the surreal and satirical realms of neo-classical Blender Fiction, filled with television shoes and flesh-filled skies. **120 pages $10**

BB-049 **"Vacation" Jeremy C. Shipp** - Blueblood Bernard Johnson leaved his boring life behind to go on The Vacation, a year-long corporate sponsored odyssey. But instead of seeing the world, Bernard is captured by terrorists, becomes a key figure in secret drug wars, and, worse, doesn't once miss his secure American Dream. **160 pages $14**

BB-053 **"Ballad of a Slow Poisoner" Andrew Goldfarb** Millford Mutterwurst sat down on a Tuesday to take his afternoon tea, and made the unpleasant discovery that his elbows were becoming flatter. **128 pages $10**

BB-055 **"Help! A Bear is Eating Me" Mykle Hansen** - The bizarro, heartwarming, magical tale of poor planning, hubris and severe blood loss... **150 pages $11**

BB-056 **"Piecemeal June" Jordan Krall** - A man falls in love with a living sex doll, but with love comes danger when her creator comes after her with crab-squid assassins. **90 pages $9**

BB-058 "The Overwhelming Urge" Andersen Prunty - A collection of bizarro tales by Andersen Prunty. **150 pages $11**

BB-059 "Adolf in Wonderland" Carlton Mellick III - A dreamlike adventure that takes a young descendant of Adolf Hitler's design and sends him down the rabbit hole into a world of imperfection and disorder. **180 pages $11**

BB-061 "Ultra Fuckers" Carlton Mellick III - Absurdist suburban horror about a couple who enter an upper middle class gated community but can't find their way out. **108 pages $9**

BB-062 "House of Houses" Kevin L. Donihe - An odd man wants to marry his house. Unfortunately, all of the houses in the world collapse at the same time in the Great House Holocaust. Now he must travel to House Heaven to find his departed fiancee. **172 pages $11**

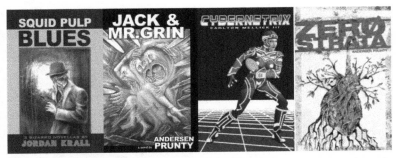

BB-064 "Squid Pulp Blues" Jordan Krall - In these three bizarro-noir novellas, the reader is thrown into a world of murderers, drugs made from squid parts, deformed gun-toting veterans, and a mischievous apocalyptic donkey. **204 pages $12**

BB-065 "Jack and Mr. Grin" Andersen Prunty - "When Mr. Grin calls you can hear a smile in his voice. Not a warm and friendly smile, but the kind that seizes your spine in fear. You don't need to pay your phone bill to hear it. That smile is in every line of Prunty's prose." - Tom Bradley. **208 pages $12**

BB-066 "Cybernetrix" Carlton Mellick III - What would you do if your normal everyday world was slowly mutating into the video game world from Tron? **212 pages $12**

BB-072 "Zerostrata" Andersen Prunty - Hansel Nothing lives in a tree house, suffers from memory loss, has a very eccentric family, and falls in love with a woman who runs naked through the woods every night. **144 pages $11**

BB-073 "The Egg Man" Carlton Mellick III - It is a world where humans reproduce like insects. Children are the property of corporations, and having an enormous ten-foot brain implanted into your skull is a grotesque sexual fetish. Mellick's industrial urban dystopia is one of his darkest and grittiest to date. **184 pages $11**

BB-074 "Shark Hunting in Paradise Garden" Cameron Pierce - A group of strange humanoid religious fanatics travel back in time to the Garden of Eden to discover it is invested with hundreds of giant flying maneating sharks. **150 pages $10**

BB-075 "Apeshit" Carlton Mellick III - Friday the 13th meets Visitor Q. Six hipster teens go to a cabin in the woods inhabited by a deformed killer. An incredibly fucked-up parody of B-horror movies with a bizarro slant. **192 pages $12**

BB-076 "Fuckers of Everything on the Crazy Shitting Planet of the Vomit At smosphere" Mykle Hansen - Three bizarro satires. Monster Cocks, Journey to the Center of Agnes Cuddlebottom, and Crazy Shitting Planet. **228 pages $12**

BB-077 "The Kissing Bug" Daniel Scott Buck - In the tradition of Roald Dahl, Tim Burton, and Edward Gorey, comes this bizarro anti-war children's story about a bohemian conenose kissing bug who falls in love with a human woman. **116 pages $10**

BB-078 "MachoPoni" Lotus Rose - It's My Little Pony... *Bizarro* style! A long time ago Poniworld was split in two. On one side of the Jagged Line is the Pastel Kingdom, a magical land of music, parties, and positivity. On the other side of the Jagged Line is Dark Kingdom inhabited by an army of undead ponies. **148 pages $11**

BB-079 "The Faggiest Vampire" Carlton Mellick III - A Roald Dahl-esque children's story about two faggy vampires who partake in a mustache competition to find out which one is truly the faggiest. **104 pages $10**

BB-080 "Sky Tongues" Gina Ranalli - The autobiography of Sky Tongues, the biracial hermaphrodite actress with tongues for fingers. Follow her strange life story as she rises from freak to fame. **204 pages $12**

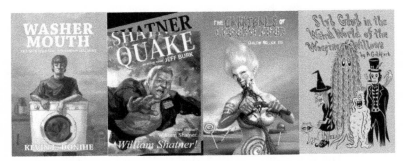

BB-081 "Washer Mouth" Kevin L. Donihe - A washing machine becomes human and pursues his dream of meeting his favorite soap opera star. **244 pages $11**

BB-082 "Shatnerquake" Jeff Burk - All of the characters ever played by William Shatner are suddenly sucked into our world. Their mission: hunt down and destroy the real William Shatner. **100 pages $10**

BB-083 "The Cannibals of Candyland" Carlton Mellick III - There exists a race of cannibals that are made of candy. They live in an underground world made out of candy. One man has dedicated his life to killing them all. **170 pages $11**

BB-084 "Slub Glub in the Weird World of the Weeping Willows" Andrew Goldfarb - The charming tale of a blue glob named Slub Glub who helps the weeping willows whose tears are flooding the earth. There are also hyenas, ghosts, and a voodoo priest **100 pages $10**

BB-085 "Super Fetus" Adam Pepper - Try to abort this fetus and he'll kick your ass! **104 pages $10**

BB-086 "Fistful of Feet" Jordan Krall - A bizarro tribute to spaghetti westerns, featuring Cthulhu-worshipping Indians, a woman with four feet, a crazed gunman who is obsessed with sucking on candy, Syphilis-ridden mutants, sexually transmitted tattoos, and a house devoted to the freakiest fetishes. **228 pages $12**

BB-087 "Ass Goblins of Auschwitz" Cameron Pierce - It's Monty Python meets Nazi exploitation in a surreal nightmare as can only be imagined by Bizarro author Cameron Pierce. **104 pages $10**

BB-088 "Silent Weapons for Quiet Wars" Cody Goodfellow - "This is high-end psychological surrealist horror meets bottom-feeding low-life crime in a techno-thrilling science fiction world full of Lovecraft and magic..." -John Skipp **212 pages $12**

BB-089 "Warrior Wolf Women of the Wasteland" Carlton Mellick III
Road Warrior Werewolves versus McDonaldland Mutants...post-apocalyptic fiction has never been quite like this. **316 pages $13**

BB-090 "Cursed" Jeremy C Shipp - The story of a group of characters who believe they are cursed and attempt to figure out who cursed them and why. A tale of stylish absurdism and suspenseful horror. **218 pages $15**

BB-091 "Super Giant Monster Time" Jeff Burk - A tribute to choose your own adventures and Godzilla movies. Will you escape the giant monsters that are rampaging the fuck out of your city and shit? Or will you join the mob of alien-controlled punk rockers causing chaos in the streets? What happens next depends on you. **188 pages $12**

BB-092 "Perfect Union" Cody Goodfellow - "Cronenberg's THE FLY on a grand scale: human/insect gene-spliced body horror, where the human hive politics are as shocking as the gore." -John Skipp. **272 pages $13**

BB-093 "Sunset with a Beard" Carlton Mellick III - 14 stories of surreal science fiction. **200 pages $12**

BB-094 "My Fake War" Andersen Prunty - The absurd tale of an unlikely soldier forced to fight a war that, quite possibly, does not exist. It's Rambo meets Waiting for Godot in this subversive satire of American values and the scope of the human imagination. **128 pages $11**

BB-095 "Lost in Cat Brain Land" Cameron Pierce - Sad stories from a surreal world. A fascist mustache, the ghost of Franz Kafka, a desert inside a dead cat. Primordial entities mourn the death of their child. The desperate serve tea to mysterious creatures. A hopeless romantic falls in love with a pterodactyl. And much more. **152 pages $11**

BB-096 "The Kobold Wizard's Dildo of Enlightenment +2" Carlton Mellick III - A Dungeons and Dragons parody about a group of people who learn they are only made up characters in an AD&D campaign and must find a way to resist their nerdy teenaged players and retarded dungeon master in order to survive. 232 **pages $12**

BB-097 **"My Heart Said No, but the Camera Crew Said Yes!" Bradley Sands -** A collection of short stories that are crammed with the delightfully odd and the scurrilously silly. **140 pages $13**

BB-098 **"A Hundred Horrible Sorrows of Ogner Stump" Andrew Goldfarb -** Goldfarb's acclaimed comic series. A magical and weird journey into the horrors of everyday life. **164 pages $11**

BB-099 **"Pickled Apocalypse of Pancake Island" Cameron Pierce** A demented fairy tale about a pickle, a pancake, and the apocalypse. **102 pages $8**

BB-100 **"Slag Attack" Andersen Prunty -** Slag Attack features four visceral, noir stories about the living, crawling apocalypse. A slag is what survivors are calling the slug-like maggots raining from the sky, burrowing inside people, and hollowing out their flesh and their sanity. **148 pages $11**

BB-101 **"Slaughterhouse High" Robert Devereaux -** A place where schools are built with secret passageways, rebellious teens get zippers installed in their mouths and genitals, and once a year, on that special night, one couple is slaughtered and the bits of their bodies are kept as souvenirs. **304 pages $13**

BB-102 **"The Emerald Burrito of Oz" John Skipp & Marc Levinthal** OZ IS REAL! Magic is real! The gate is really in Kansas! And America is finally allowing Earth tourists to visit this weird-ass, mysterious land. But when Gene of Los Angeles heads off for summer vacation in the Emerald City, little does he know that a war is brewing...a war that could destroy both worlds. **280 pages $13**

BB-103 **"The Vegan Revolution... with Zombies" David Agranoff** When there's no more meat in hell, the vegans will walk the earth. **160 pages $11**

BB-104 **"The Flappy Parts" Kevin L Donihe -** Poems about bunnies, LSD, and police abuse. You know, things that matter. 132 **pages $11**

BB-105 **"Sorry I Ruined Your Orgy" Bradley Sands** - Bizarro humorist Bradley Sands returns with one of the strangest, most hilarious collections of the year. **130 pages $11**

BB-106 **"Mr. Magic Realism" Bruce Taylor** - Like Golden Age science fiction comics written by Freud, *Mr. Magic Realism* is a strange, insightful adventure that spans the furthest reaches of the galaxy, exploring the hidden caverns in the hearts and minds of men, women, aliens, and biomechanical cats. **152 pages $11**

BB-107 **"Zombies and Shit" Carlton Mellick III** - "Battle Royale" meets "Return of the Living Dead." Mellick's bizarro tribute to the zombie genre. **308 pages $13**

BB-108 **"The Cannibal's Guide to Ethical Living" Mykle Hansen** - Over a five star French meal of fine wine, organic vegetables and human flesh, a lunatic delivers a witty, chilling, disturbingly sane argument in favor of eating the rich.. **184 pages $11**

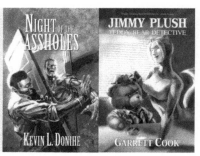

BB-109 **"Starfish Girl" Athena Villaverde** - In a post-apocalyptic underwater dome society, a girl with a starfish growing from her head and an assassin with sea anenome hair are on the run from a gang of mutant fish men. **160 pages $11**

BB-110 **"Lick Your Neighbor" Chris Genoa** - Mutant ninjas, a talking whale, kung fu masters, maniacal pilgrims, and an alcoholic clown populate Chris Genoa's surreal, darkly comical and unnerving reimagining of the first Thanksgiving. **303 pages $13**

BB-111 **"Night of the Assholes" Kevin L. Donihe** - A plague of assholes is infecting the countryside. Normal everyday people are transforming into jerks, snobs, dicks, and douchebags. And they all have only one purpose: to make your life a living hell.. **192 pages $11**

BB-112 **"Jimmy Plush, Teddy Bear Detective" Garrett Cook** - Hardboiled cases of a private detective trapped within a teddy bear body. **180 pages $11**